Baby, I'm Yours

CATHERINE MANN

SILHOUETTE®

DESIRE™

First published in Great Britain 2007
Large Print edition 2007
Silhouette Books Limited, Eton House,
18-24 Paradise Road, Richmond, Surrey, TW9 1SR

© Catherine Mann 2006

ISBN-13: 978 0 373 40154 3
ISBN-10:   0 373 40154 X

Set in Times Roman 17 on 21 pt.
36-0207-41149

Printed and bound in Great Britain
by Antony Rowe Ltd, Chippenham, Wiltshire

Prologue

"**A**h, hell, it broke."

The second the stunned words fell out of Vic Jansen's mouth he wanted to recall them for something more composed. But what was the mannerly way to tell the naked woman straddling his lap that their birth control had suffered a catastrophic failure?

This wasn't supposed to happen to two over-thirty adults.

"What do you mean, *it broke?*" Claire's horrified whisper steamed over his chest as they sat tangled together. The steamy gust stirred a fire down south when he should have been long past recovery after their weekend of marathon sex.

Lifting her off and to the side, Vic squinted in the darkness to see his friend of six months and lover of three days. Years of veterinary practice had prepped him for hostile horses and spitting-mad cats, but at the moment he felt damned unprepared to cope with Claire McDermott and a possible pregnancy.

Coping with memories of the daughter he'd lost proved even tougher. He shoved aside images of pigtails, Barbie dolls—funeral wreaths.

"Exactly what I said." He swiped a wrist across his forehead, flinging aside sweat in spite of the forty-degree weather of a southern January evening. "The condom tore."

"There's absolutely no way it should have broken." Panic pitching her voice higher, breathier, Claire snatched her dress from beside her feet and clutched it to her bare breasts he wanted to unveil and kiss all over again. "I know they only have a ninety-six percent reliability factor, but that four percent encompasses idiots who don't know how to use the things."

"Well, lady, tonight we two idiots just blew those stats right out of the water—as it were." Vic gripped the steel rim of the bass boat, the plastic fishing chair chilling his skin. "Be still, will ya? You're going to tip us over."

Claire puffed a breath of air upward, blowing away a lank lock dangling in her face, puffed again, then finally combed shaking fingers through her tousled caramel-colored hair. He couldn't let himself think about threading his hands through her silky strands as he held her curvy body against his or he would lose his focus.

She untangled a gelatinous lure and flicked it onto the tackle box. "Are you sure you didn't catch the condom on a hook or something?"

"Jeez, Claire." Vic clasped her shoulders, her soft scented skin sending a fresh jolt of heat through him. "Don't you think I would know if I had a hook in it?"

"Good point." She dodged the cooler, leaning over the seat, which displayed a flash of tempting flesh before she straightened, her lacy bra and panties in hand. "That's the last time you get to supply birth control."

"I feel compelled to point out that it's one I snagged from your bedside table—" he tugged on his jeans "—since we'd used up mine."

The slap and crash of waves against the shore filled the silence while Claire shimmied into her underwear. Vic grimaced at her extended quiet. Theirs had been an unlikely friendship of opposites—classic Claire with all her pretty lace, and he with his flannel, rough-around-the-edges ways. But a friendship he'd come to value in the past six months since he'd sold his vet practice in North

Dakota and relocated to Charleston, South Carolina, away from all reminders of his daughter and ex-wife.

Yet, in spite of his vow for a rootless existence living on a sailboat, more and more often he'd found himself walking across the marina dock to Beachcombers restaurant for Claire's home-cooked meal, a glass of sweet tea—and her smile.

Claire suddenly seemed overly interested in how her dress buttoned up the front. "Those condoms in my bedside table were old. I, uh, haven't been with anyone for a long time."

"Really?"

She swayed toward him. "Really."

Damn, she never failed to capsize his control with her unexpected moments of vulnerability peeking through her unflappable shield. Vic pulled her against his chest. She resisted half-heartedly, then relented.

He smoothed his hands over her back, down her spine while resisting the tempting curve of her bottom. "I don't have any diseases you need to worry about, if that makes you feel better."

"A little." Her full lips curved into a hesitant smile against his skin. "Me neither, by the way, no surprise given my non-existent sex life…up to now."

She eased free, the boat lurching in response. Once steadied, Claire slipped her feet into her pumps.

"What are the odds, given the timing of your cycle?"

"You don't want to know."

"Are you sure? Never mind." Stupid question. The risk of having another kid scared the pants right back off him, but Claire deserved some kind of reassurance. "Let's take this a day at a time. There's no need to get in a frenzy about something that may not even happen. We'll discuss it when and if we need to, but I'll be there for you."

Claire stared back at him in the dark,

waiting…for what? Finally, she shook her head. "Like you said, we'll discuss it later."

She snatched up her sweater and leaped from the boat onto the asphalt.

Sliding open the garage door, she revealed the marina parking lot and her restaurant/home up the hill overlooking docked crafts bobbing in the harbor.

They'd been on their way to his forty-two-foot sailboat when they'd been delayed by a spontaneous make-out session against a string of garages for marina residents. And hey, since he owned the truck and bass boat inside, why wait?

Zipping his pants, he tracked her sweet butt hauling up the planked walkway toward the two-story restaurant she co-owned with her sisters. A few leftover Christmas lights illuminated her double-time progress away from him. He considered simply letting her go and giving them both some space. But even as frustrated as he was over her deep freeze, he owed Claire for challenging him back to life after years of numbed emotions.

That meant he couldn't let her walk away scared.

Snagging his shirt, he vaulted over the side of the boat. He stuffed his arms through the flannel softness that now carried Claire's lilac scent, along with a few ripped buttonholes from her frantic hands.

"Hold on." He dashed after her, the tails of his open shirt flapping behind him.

The need for a better end to their weekend raked aside everything else, including shoes. He thudded barefoot past the marina office onto her property, across the patchy sandy lawn.

Toes darn-near frostbitten, Vic made it to her front porch a hairbreadth behind her. He braced a hand just beside her and rested his cheek against the back of her head, nuzzling against her tangled hair. She tensed, but she didn't move, gasping in the humid night.

His brain scrambled for the right words, a way to shift them back to what they'd shared before he'd ruined it by taking her to bed—or to his boat. "I know you needed me to say something, and I fell short of the mark."

The tense brace of her shoulders sent alarms through him. Claire was beyond upset. She was in a blind panic. What fears of her own was she carrying around that she hadn't shared with him any more than he'd told her about his?

And what a time to realize they hadn't been friends in any meaningful manner after all. Just meal-sharing acquaintances who'd gotten naked together. "God almighty, lady, you're the most exasperating and incredible woman I've ever met. But I'm not very good at the pretty words."

Slowly, she turned, tilting her chin defensively. She reached, her hand hovering between them almost touching his bare chest, but settling on the open shirt instead. "I need to be alone right now. But I promise I'll let you know if I'm…"

She didn't need to finish. Her shuttered expression said it all. They couldn't go back to what little they'd had. Disappointment chugged through him, more than he would have expected three short days ago.

His hands slid from her face. "Okay, I'll be waiting to hear from you then. You know where to find me."

He stepped back from the porch, Claire, her smile. Déjà vu swept over him as she sprinted up the steps and into her antebellum restaurant/home. How many times would he watch people he cared about fade from his life?

Damned if numb wasn't better after all.

One

Charleston, S.C.:
Three-and-a-half months later

"Claire, if you handle a man with as much finesse as you're using on that swizzle stick, it's no wonder you sleep alone."

Tucked in a corner of her bustling restaurant kitchen, Claire surrendered the pitcher of mint juleps to her sister before she sloshed ice onto the counter. "Swizzle stick? Either you're more innocent than you let on or you've just insulted some poor guy in a big—or would that be little?—way."

"Guilty as charged," Starr answered ambiguously as she assumed control of the fragrant mixed drink, sprinkling fresh mint leaves on top before passing it over to a waitress.

Claire picked through her herb garden in the open window while stifling the urge to blurt how she'd handled one man a little too well three-and-a-half months ago. Now, she had a permanent reminder of that weekend-long sensual feast last January.

Her hands shook as she snagged the empty bowl for parsley sprigs. "I'm too busy for a love life."

Today in particular, she had enough on her plate feeding the Beachcombers Bar and Grill Saturday lunch crowd while prepping for the packed week of catering events. Even with the help of her two foster sisters, co-owners in the business, soon she would be busier still with a baby on her hip. Not that she intended to let that information leak to the kitchen full of staff clanging pots and filling orders.

She had to tell the baby's daddy first.

And she would—after this week passed and she could compose herself with a long bubble bath. She'd only been delaying telling Vic out of practicality. Right? Ever reasonable, she always made the practical decision.

Except for once, and that whopper had landed her in the same shoes as her pregnant unwed mama. However, unlike her mama, Claire was blessed with resources and choices. No one would force *her* to hand over her child.

Starr rolled silverware inside napkins with lightning speed, pouring more of that frenetic energy into swaying along with beach music thrumming through the sound system. "Who said anything about love? I'm only talking about you getting out more, dating. Pencil in some fun time on that perfectly ordered daily agenda of yours."

Even Starr's dark hair snapped with energy, curls straining to pop free from the constraining long braid while Claire felt more like one of the wrung-out rags in the industrial sink.

"I *am* enjoying life since I love my work." Huffing a lank wisp off her forehead, she scooched closer to the counter to make way for a waiter balancing a cornbread-stuffed catfish special.

Vic's favorite.

Her hand drifted downward. She stopped shy of her stomach, shooting a quick glance at her younger foster sister. Starr's eagle eye missed nothing, a skill gained from her time on the streets before she landed in the same foster home as Claire and their other foster sister, Ashley.

Claire eyed the swinging door with longing. If only she could dash out of the humid kitchen, away from too-discerning questions. But she couldn't risk leaving for at least an hour since Vic Jansen had parked his fine butt in her dining room for lunch.

"Work," Starr snorted. "Work won't sizzle you with a look or have you ready to climb out of your skin after a kiss."

Do not think of Vic. Vic's kiss. Vic's hard-muscled body under her hands, his tall strength covering her with such seductive gentleness and utter confidence in every deep stroke.

Uh-oh. Hormone alert.

Claire clipped a fistful of chives, ran them under the faucet and fanned them along the butcher block. "Cooking is relaxing." Order in the middle of chaos. "I had a blast decorating that baby shower cake last night, listening to the spring rain patter."

Until she'd fallen asleep in her frosting. Claire whacked the chives.

Work might not launch her hormones into overdrive, but it also didn't confuse her like

the man eating in the next room. She needed reliability in her life, especially now. Even with
its shoestring budget, her business provided
more stability than any man with broad shoulders that screamed to her fingers *explore me...*

A crash echoed from the narrow hall.

Claire winced at the clatter of shattering china.
Superstitious Starr snatched a saltshaker from
the counter and pitched a pinch over her shoulder.

Another reason to keep quiet about the baby.
Claire refused to let anyone label this pregnancy the latest in a gosh-awful string of bad
luck alongside a leaky roof. A broken water
pipe. A rotten board giving way on a porch she
could have sworn was in pristine condition. All
expensive repairs she could ill-afford if she
wanted to keep the business.

Jeez, some days she almost wondered if
somebody was out to ruin her—or her house.

Not a chance would she let that happen. This
historic old wreck was the only real home she'd

ever had. Her biological mother had skipped from apartment to apartment, shelters sometimes too, depending on her finances. Tina McDermott had tried her best to provide for her daughter, but as a seventeen-year-old single mother booted out by her parents before graduation… well, options sucked.

The Department of Social Services had removed Claire at age eight, after discovering Tina was leaving her child alone to work the midnight shift at a truck stop. The Department of Social Services had placed Claire in the care of a kooky, wonderful old woman with a dilapidated antebellum mansion, no money, and a half dozen foster daughters. Many more came and went, placed with permanent families. All but Starr, Ashley and her. When "Aunt" Libby died just over a year ago, she'd left the house to the three of them. Starting a restaurant together was a near-impossible dream, but one they held tenaciously.

Starr passed a basketful of rolled napkins to a busboy before turning back to Claire. "Maybe I'm being a little pushy today because I'm worried about you pulling off all these parties. No offense, but you look like hell."

"Not a problem. You're talking to me. Remember?" She picked up her knife and resumed chopping. "The Queen of Anal Retentive. Who wouldn't look like hell during a busy lunch hour?"

She couldn't control the exhaustion of her pregnancy, but she prided herself on her organizational skills, a matter of survival when she'd been living with Tina.

Claire chopped faster. Multiple orders echoed up to the high ceiling, along with the familiar clamor of clanging dishes, shouted calls for another pitcher of sweet tea.

Vic drank her sweet tea by the gallons.

Argh! Claire stared down at the pulverized chives. Couldn't she go at least ten minutes without thinking about the guy? Kind of tough to manage with an ever-present reminder of him in her belly frothing up morning sickness.

Morning sickness quickly segued into afternoon sickness, thanks to a lack of sleep and the clam chowder steaming aromas and heat from a ten-gallon stainless steel pot. No wonder she looked like hell. She felt like hell.

Crash.

Starr grabbed the saltshaker.

Claire made a beeline for the door before the new waiter destroyed every dish in the place. She would just stay well clear of Vic. He had no reason to seek her out since a month after their encounter in his fishing boat, she'd told him she wasn't pregnant. Which she'd genuinely believed after a spotting episode.

A trip to the doctor for her stomach flu shocked the dickens out of her, then scared her silly because did spotting mean her baby was in danger? And suddenly the baby wasn't an accident or burden, but rather a little person she wanted so very much.

Sprinting for the hall, Claire hollered back over her shoulder, "Call Ashley and tell her we need help after she's done with classes, please."

Their reclusive younger sister preferred to hover in the background, but she wouldn't stay secluded in her dorm while their business went under.

Claire dodged a busboy with a tub of dirty plates on her way through the kitchen into the hall. A quick mental floor-plan check assured her Vic would be safely out of sight since he always chose the same corner table, number eight.

She screeched to a halt inches away from a mountain of broken china mixed with fried okra and baked chicken.

An overwhelmed waiter with a smooshed corn muffin in hand stared up at her. "Table eight needs to place an order."

And the bad luck just kept coming.

Where was a shaker full of salt when a down-on-her-luck girl needed it?

"Pass the salt, will ya?" Vic asked his brother-in-law, wondering how many more times he would have to come here before Claire finally talked to him. Face to face, and not in some terse little voice mail message…

No need to worry. You're off the hook. I'm not pregnant.

Great news. Back to his rootless existence living on his sailboat, as different from his old North Dakota prairie world as possible. Totally free. Except he had these two regrets.

And one of them was walking across the packed dining room of the best-loved new restaurant in Charleston. Right toward his table.

Claire. Her name whispered in his mind like the spring breeze drifting through the open windows, rustling the fishing nets tacked to whitewashed walls. She looked so pretty and fresh in her loose jean dress cinched tight by an apron. Ceiling fans clicked overhead, lifting a strand of her caramel hair free from her gold hair clamp.

She'd been the only thing keeping him going through that *other* regret. Until he'd messed it up by sleeping with her, then letting his commitment-phobe mindset show.

Claire glided to a stop, her dress swishing a gentle caress against his leg that sparked a not-so-gentle jolt of desire straight to his groin conveniently camouflaged by a tablecloth.

"Good afternoon, gentlemen, welcome to Beachcombers," she drawled, molasses-sweet tones sliding over his hungry senses. "What can I get for you this afternoon?"

How about a plate of forgiveness?

Except from her closed expression he could see it wasn't on her menu. Her chocolate-colored gaze met his dead-on and damned if he didn't want to add a few more regrets to his list.

She pulled a pad and pencil from her apron pocket. "The specials are cornbread-stuffed catfish and chicken-fried steak, followed with a slice of chocolate pecan pie. Could I start you out with an order of the house special barbecue wings?"

If only they could back up to where they'd been before. He missed those uncomplicated hours of staying after closing, drinking her iced tea and talking to fill the lonely evenings before he returned to his sailboat.

Hang tough and place the order, champ. "The catfish sounds fine, Claire. Thanks."

Nodding, she turned to his brother-in-law, Bo Rokowsky, baching it with him this afternoon. Vic thanked heaven every day his sister, Paige, had found a great guy like Bo after her crummy first marriage, but he also marveled at her ability to put her neck on the block a second time around.

Vic watched the way Claire's full lips moved

as she listed other house specialties. He wondered why he kept torturing himself by coming here trying to talk to her. He would have more luck getting a response from the stuffed fish over the doors.

Women like Claire McDermott who carried the scent of fresh-baked rolls and happily ever after didn't need a guy like him in her life or in her towering four-poster bed. He'd tried the gold band and white picket fence gig. He'd even thought he and Sonya had built a rock-solid marriage, only to have the whole thing crumble when they'd needed each other most.

Which brought him to his first and greatest regret—looking away for five freaking seconds to rebait his hook while Emma was wading. There had been a couple of other dads and kids—and one small sinkhole in the shallow riverbank.

Nope, he was through with home and hearth, nearing forty and set in his bachelor life. Work at the vet clinic offered a welcome distraction, and time with his niece took care of any paternal leanings that somehow managed to survive inside his battered heart.

Waiting while Bo read over the menu, again, Vic reeled his gaze away from Claire and fixed it on safer subjects. The gauzy curtains gusting in a briny breeze and the sound of sail lines snapping and pinging against masts.

None of which helped since he couldn't ignore the heat of Claire standing twelve inches away.

A cellphone chirped, tugging his gaze back to the room. At least a dozen people reached into pockets or grabbed for purses, but Bo whipped the winning phone from his jean pocket. He glanced at the faceplate and pushed back his wooden chair.

"It's Paige. I need to take this outside where I can hear better." Bo slapped Vic on the shoulder as he passed. "Go ahead and order for me?"

"Sure," Vic agreed, not that it mattered since the former "player" was already heading outside for the wraparound porch, so sappy gone on Paige and family life it made Vic remember lost dreams.

Silence swelled, exaggerated all the more by the increasing clamor of boat traffic outside. Clanking utensils inside. Tables full of other people apparently having no trouble at all finding things to say to each other.

Claire doodled on the corner of her pad for three clicks of the ceiling fans before flipping the pad closed. The familiar Claire returned with her smile. "Do you think this could be any more awkward?"

Vic welcomed the laugh. Perhaps he'd been worrying for nothing. Time might have fixed things for him. "Maybe if all our families joined us."

Having her nutty—overprotective—sisters around would definitely make any situation more uncomfortable.

Claire jabbed a thumb over her shoulder

toward the hall. "Starr is in the kitchen and Bo will be here again in a minute. Does that count?"

"Well, there you have it, then." He leaned his chair back, arms crossed. "We've faced the worst."

"It can only get better, right?"

Man, he hoped so.

He eased his chair down onto all fours. "How have you been?"

"Fine. Busy." She toyed with the waistband of her creamy apron, Beachcombers scrolled on the breast pocket, underlined with a stitched string of tiny shells and footprints he itched to trace.

The waistband accentuated the gentle fullness of her breasts in the Beachcombers jean-and-white theme wear. Fuller than he remembered. And at his eye level.

His mouth dried right up.

Vic took a long swallow of his iced tea before setting the glass back on the table. He had to clear the air or dock his sailboat elsewhere. The boat had seemed like such a great idea when he'd sold off his vet practice and old family home full of memories back in North Dakota. He'd followed his sister and her kid to Charleston when she'd married a local flyboy.

Securing a job at a local veterinary clinic had been easy enough with his Cornell credentials. The boat was all about being a bachelor in this harbor town and able to pull up anchor and sail off for a weekend when memories got to be too much for him. A much better option than drinking away the memories, which he'd started doing too often in his North Dakota home that echoed with childish giggles and tiny footsteps.

Except three-and-a-half months ago, instead of drinking, he'd screwed up and lost himself in Claire on a day when the memories dogged him. The day Emma would have been nine years old.

He'd stayed late at the restaurant to talk with Claire. Too late, and by bottom of the third glass of tea, he'd been cupping *her* sweet bottom in his hands as they plastered themselves to each other in an out-of-control kiss.

He owed Claire an apology. If she wouldn't let him deliver it in private, he would settle for their semiprivate table. "Claire? Why don't you sit until Bo gets back? You look exhausted."

And she did, so much so he questioned the wisdom of hashing this out now.

"Exhausted? Seems the Jansen charm's in limited supply today," she drawled.

Still, she sat. Apparently exhaustion won over pride.

"Even dog-tired you still put other women in the dark."

"Ah, the charm's back." Claire shuffled mixed-up sugar and artificial sweetener packets in the tiny basket, resuming order. Pink on one side. White on the other.

He remembered well what those competent hands could do to his self-control. "Not charm. Truth."

One elegant finger nudged the lantern center-piece an inch to the left. "Things are hectic. I'm shorthanded here and the wedding's coming up."

"Wedding?" Jealousy bit. Hard.

"I meant, the rehearsal dinner that I'm catering next Friday and three baby showers before then."

"Oh, right." He knew that, and he'd forgotten just by looking at her hands.

"These catering gigs are important for the business." She folded her hands on the table, a small burn staining the tip of one finger.

A protective urge left him itching to do something, to help her. Not that independent Claire would let him do jack. She had her foster sisters to lean on anytime, and undoubtedly a guy someday, too. She should spend her time with a man who could give her a wedding of her own to plan.

Which wasn't him.

Vic shut down senseless regrets, unrolled his silverware from the napkin and plastered on his best life-suits-me-fine smile. "I'm sure everything will go smoothly with you organizing it." He dropped his napkin across one thigh. "Just bring Bo the chicken-fried steak."

She scraped her chair back, obviously ready to run. "Sure, I'll send that right out with Starr."

A clearing throat sounded from behind Vic. He couldn't decide whether or not to be grateful for his brother-in-law's return.

Bo tucked the cell phone in his jeans pocket, eyeing the two of them with suspicion—and dangerous speculation. "No chicken-fried steak for me. I'm cutting back on cholesterol. Could you hang around for a minute more while I look over the menu again?"

Staring up at the indecisive customer she currently longed to strangle, Claire stifled a frustrated scream. The bad luck just kept rolling in at a time when she needed to bolt for the kitchen, far away from the temptation to tell Vic everything now.

Or worse yet, crawl into his lap and all over him. Now wouldn't that go over well with the Saturday lunchtime clientele?

Claire launched to her feet. Too fast. She grabbed the chairback for support as her stomach rose to her throat without warning. If Vic's brother-in-law didn't make up his mind soon so she could leave, she was going to toss what little she'd eaten all over Vic's work boots. Big work boots.

No little swizzle stick.

"Gentlemen, how about I give you a while longer to look over the menu? I'll send someone out to take your order in a few minutes."

Please, please, please, Starr, arrive soon.

"No need," Bo insisted. "It'll just take a second, darlin', and I may have some questions." He studied the menu.

For the third time.

Was this guy torturing her on purpose?

Claire flipped open her pad again and doodled tiny baby bottles along the edges to keep from looking at Vic. She dreaded her upcoming conversation with him, but she couldn't hide the pregnancy much longer. Already, her apron pulled tighter around her waist, and she'd seen his eyes linger on her swollen breasts.

Overly sensitive breasts that currently tingled for the touch of his talented tongue.

How would the footloose bachelor react to the news that he would soon be a daddy? Especially when she could tell he wasn't over his divorce.

The green-eyed monster nipped her, then turned a sad shade of blue as she thought about the little girl he'd lost and how this would make him think of her all the more.

Claire's aching maternal heart clenched in sympathy. She didn't know the details beyond gossip since Vic never talked about his past, a telling silence. The rumor mill held that his daughter drowned and his marriage dissolved as a result.

The green-blue monster turned fiery red to confront the woman who'd walked out on Vic.

Jeez, it wasn't like they were even dating. Just friends who'd fallen victim to a nocturnal chat and loneliness for one impulsive weekend. Okay, a three-day weekend where they didn't sleep much. Then the whole condom accident cut everything short because for some reason she'd kept the old box around from her brief engagement four years prior.

At thirty, she should be wiser now about her relationship track record. But Vic had a dangerous effect on her self-control.

Bo slapped the menu shut, jerking Claire back to the present. She poised her pencil, ready to write and run.

"Could you list some of the other house specials?"

She inhaled three slow breaths and willed her stomach not to swell in the eons it seemed it would take this military aviator to make up his mind. "Baby back ribs. Baby artichoke salad. Baked chicken served with baby potatoes and glazed baby carrots."

Baby? Even the menu was out to get her today. She moved on to safer foods.

"Or pulled-chicken pecan salad on a crisp bed," she pushed aside thoughts of beds with Vic sprawled across crisp white sheets, "a bed of iceberg lettuce."

Ice. Yes, cool, chilling thoughts.

"Hmm." Bo tapped his menu against his chin. "What else?"

Patience, she reminded herself. A mother needed to have patience. "One of our house specialties is country ham." Would their baby have Vic's blond hair and his blue eyes? "With blue-eye, uh, I mean redeye gravy."

"I'll take the chicken-fried steak after all."

Chicken certainly seemed appropriate for the day since she felt like a great big coward. "Ooh-kay. One chicken-fried steak and a cornbread catfish coming right up."

Plucking a folded napkin from her pocket, Claire dabbed the sweat from her brow and willed away the dizziness. Surely it had more to do with her lack of lunch than with the rugged hunk sucking all the oxygen from the room. She pocketed her notepad in her apron and spun away on her heels.

Too fast.

The room tipped.

Thrusting out a hand, Claire stared help-lessly at the floor growing closer and could only think how apparently her bad luck wasn't over for the day.

Two

With lightning reflexes gained from years of dodging potentially lethal horse kicks, Vic shot out of his chair. He scooped Claire up before she hit the hardwood floor.

He bent on one knee, Claire cradled to his chest where his heart pumped. Too fast. Warm and soft, she sagged against him, with dark circles under her eyes. Her head lolled on his shoulder.

"Claire? Talk to me." What if she was actually

sick? He pressed two fingers to her throat and found a steady pulse.

Thank God.

She sighed and snuggled closer, her eyes closed while chairs scraped back throughout the dining room. Footsteps vibrated the floor. Overhead lights dimmed as curious patrons circled, not that he could see anything other than Claire's pale face at the moment.

Why couldn't there have been a doctor in today's diners? His medical training wasn't worth jack at the moment.

The mass parted as a wiry woman pushed through with a nervous energy that rivaled a hummingbird on Mountain Dew. Claire's sister Starr fluttered to a stop.

"Move on over, people, and let her breathe." Not a soul dared disobey the scrappy five feet of frenetic will and wildly escaping hair. "What happened?"

"I have no idea. She just keeled over." And

shaved at least two years off his life. His heart hadn't slammed this hard against his ribs when he'd jumped a fence to avoid getting gored by an angry, recently castrated bull. "She doesn't seem to be hurt. I caught her before she hit the floor."

Starr nodded, rising. "Good. Good. Now put all those hard-working muscles to good use and let's move her someplace quiet while we decide whether to call EMS."

Vic gathered Claire more securely in his arms and stood, unable to resist savoring the soft swell of her breasts against his chest, the flowery scent of her hair. And had he mentioned the swell of her breasts against his chest? Of course, Claire would likely clock him with a frying pan when she woke up.

If she woke up.

Concern cranked into high gear. He knew all too well how fragile life could be. In some distant part of his brain, Vic heard Bo speaking to him, but couldn't concentrate on anything more than Claire in his arms.

He charged around tables after Starr into the hall where waiting patrons gaped. Starr unhooked the golden rope across the stairway that kept guests from going up to the private apartment and waved him past.

Turning sideways, he sprinted up the hardwood steps to the landing and up again. Whitewashed walls gave way to faded wallpaper with cabbage roses. Claire had talked about her plans for stripping the paper in her never-ending task of renovating the house. She worked too hard. Who looked out for her?

He shut down the thought, along with others stinging him with how much this place resembled the family house he'd sold in North Dakota. Not that they actually looked alike, this one full of old southern class and his eked in prairie starkness.

But the air of *home,* he recognized well.

At the top of the stairs, Vic reached to open

the hall door leading to the living quarters, never loosening his hold on Claire. Scents of home-cooked meals gave way to the fragrance of a hundred percent *her*.

Flowers, the purple kind. Lilacs maybe? The perfume she carried on her body. On her crisp fresh sheets. A scent she'd imprinted on his memory.

Vic turned to Starr a couple of steps behind him. "Where should we go?"

"She'll be more comfortable on her bed."

Pivoting on his heel, he charged through the sitting area, down the hall, to the first room on the left.

And froze.

He shouldn't know which door led to her bedroom. Heat crawled up the back of his neck. Aw, for Pete's sake, thirty-nine was too old to blush.

He offered a belated questioning look to Starr. "Uh, is this it?"

Starr cocked her head to the side. The heat along his neck flamed a little hotter. *Busted.*

Since Starr lived in the carriage house out back and their other sister, Ashley, lived on campus at the College of Charleston neither of them had known about his weekend up here. Unless Claire had told them.

Starr's eyes narrowed before concern returned to wipe away her unspoken question. She nodded, pushing the door wide. "In here."

Memories nailed Vic. Dead on. Flattening all his defenses as surely as if he'd been the one to pitch onto the floor instead of Claire. Her mammoth four-poster bed loomed in front of him with all those gauzy things draped around the square bracket along the top. The open window rustled the filmy draping like some kind of bridal bower over her bed.

He'd spent the best seventy-two hours of his life with her there—and against that faded cabbage rose wallpaper, and on the stairs.

In his bass boat.

Behind him, Starr cleared her throat. He needed to get his head on straight and think about Claire. Carefully, he lowered her to the fluffy comforter.

Talk about reliving memories.

You're in big trouble, champ.

Vic looked over his shoulder. "Could you get a glass of water for when she wakes up?"

Furrows wrinkled Starr's forehead. "Good idea, and a cool cloth, too. Maybe a thermometer? I'll be right back."

Claire burrowed her face into the pillow as Starr's footsteps faded down the hall. Relief kicked through him so strong he almost staggered back a step.

"Vic?" she mumbled in a sleepy voice too like the one that haunted his dreams.

"Yeah, Claire. It's me." He cleared his throat along with any thoughts of Claire's waking-up voice. "You really gave us a scare down there, lady. Are you okay?"

He hoped so, because he needed to make tracks out of her place and away from her appeal before he landed next to her.

"Mmm." She shifted onto her side toward him. "Now I am."

Claire flung an arm over Vic's shoulder and toppled him forward onto her bed.

Claire snuggled into her dream, fighting consciousness just a little longer. Tingles teased along her skin as she inhaled...*man*. Strong, warm man in her bed, heavy muscled arms and legs tangled with hers.

And not just any man.

The one she'd been dreaming of having right here beside her since the first day he'd sauntered up her walkway, taut butt, broad shoulders, so much *man* even her towering entry hall could barely contain him.

Vic's pine-soap scent and steady heartbeat soothed her senses, mellowing and exciting her at the same time. She'd needed the support of his chest so much on that night. The first anniversary of Aunt Libby's death had hit her hard, especially so close after the holidays. And she'd already been stressed out by the monied bigwigs drooling over her prime piece of waterfront property, pressuring her day in and day out to sell.

Vic's steady friendship had meant a lot to her. How could she not turn to him? Comfort that night had shifted quickly to something more.

She nuzzled his neck. "Mmm. You smell so good."

And she was so sleepy.

Vic coughed.

"Really good." Her languid arms flopped around his shoulders to toy with his collar. "You feel good, too. Have I ever told you how hot your butt looks in jeans? And that faded patch in front makes me want to flatten my h—"

"Uh, Claire…"

"Yeah, Vic?" She slid a button free through warm cotton covering even warmer man.

"We need to stop."

"Don't wanna."

His wry chuckle kissed her ears as seductively as his mouth had done a few months ago. "Well, me neither, but we have to."

She didn't want to think about her groaning bank account and repairs piling up faster than she could count them, not when a much-needed nap and a warm chest waited in this bed. She fought consciousness. For just a few seconds longer she wanted to abandon Claire-logic to the boundless possibilities of dreamland. "Why should we stop?"

"Because Starr is in the next room filling a glass of water for you. She'll be walking through that door any second now."

An icy shower of realization splashed her wide awake. This wasn't a few months ago.

This was now, with Vic on her purple comforter and totally unaware of a third little person with them.

Her eyes focused simultaneously with her thoughts.

Claire shoved Vic's chest. She bolted upright just as he rolled off the mattress, work boots thumping on the braided rug as he launched to his feet.

She hitched the hem of her dress down past her knees. "What are you doing here? What am I doing here? How did we—? What were we—?"

"Stop." He kept his voice low, glancing over his shoulder at the door before continuing, "You passed out downstairs."

Memories flooded back of pitching toward the floor. Claire pressed a hand to her stomach to reassure herself life was still growing, safe, already fully seated within her heart.

Nothing seemed wrong. She just felt queasy, ops normal these days. "I passed out?"

Nodding, Vic rebuttoned his shirt. "I carried you up here afterward. Are you okay?"

No! She wanted to shout. *I'm not okay at all.* This baby left her excited and scared at once. No matter how many times she told herself she wasn't a single seventeen-year-old like her mother, she still couldn't stem fears of letting down her child.

And in the middle of all those fears rumbled a confused mishmash of emotions for the baby's father tipping her world until she couldn't see straight. Or maybe that was because all she could see was a broad set of shoulders and a gorgeous head of thick, sun-kissed hair that begged her fingers to smooth it.

Staring into eyes so blue they turned almost as purple as the lilacs on her windowsill, she wanted to tell him about their child now. She wanted him to be happy about the baby. She needed him to reassure her they would sort out reasonable plans for sharing custody.

And if by some fluke the once-bitten-twice-shy bachelor actually offered to marry her?

Not a chance. She'd been an obligation to so many people over the years. She wouldn't put that grief on her baby.

But Aunt Libby's old voice whispered in her mind that a mama would do anything for her child. Or was that her own mother's voice she could barely remember anymore? A woman who'd even been willing to climb into a trucker's cab on occasion to earn extra dollars for rent.

Claire swallowed down sympathetic tears that pooled closer to the surface these days. She'd stumbled on that tidbit of info about her mom when searching through Aunt Libby's paperwork, which included a copy of Claire's case file. All of which flooded her eyes with more tears for both mother figures in her life who had sacrificed so much for her.

Vic's arm slid around her shoulders. "Claire, baby, are you all right?"

Omigod, she couldn't think now, and she definitely couldn't talk rationally. She blinked fast. Better to speak with Vic when her emotions were steadier…and when her sister wasn't one room away.

Claire swung her legs over the side of the bed and willed the wisteria-vine pattern climbing her faded wallpaper to quit wiggling. "I'm fine. Thank you for carrying me up here so I wasn't sprawled out there for all the customers to gawk at."

"No problem. I just want to make sure you're okay." He pressed a hand to her forehead. "My specialty may be four-legged patients, but you don't feel feverish."

Uh-oh. He wanted a reason. She gripped his wrist and tried not to notice the steady pulse under her touch, the masculine bristle of hair sprinkled along his skin. His eyes met hers, held, the pulse throbbing under her fingers sped. Hers answered with a resounding *ka-thump*.

She dropped his hand. "Thanks for the medical assistance, Doctor Jansen, but this two-legged patient is only hungry. I skipped breakfast this morning." And lunch. "With the extra catering jobs, I'm putting in additional hours. It must have caught up with me."

He jammed his clenched fists in his faded jean pockets. "You should take better care of yourself."

She knew that. Already she felt like a rotten mother, but she had such a tough time asking for help. She would—in another week. "I'll be fine once I eat something."

And kept it down.

"Even a farm vet like me can see you need a nap."

"Tomorrow." She slid off the edge of the bed to her feet. "I have too much to—"

The room tipped. Her stomach roiled. Before she could blink, Vic braced her shoulders and sat her on the bed. He gripped the back of her neck and eased her forward. She dropped her head between her knees. Her notepad thudded to the floor. She would retrieve it after she found air.

"Deep breaths. Slowly. It's okay," Vic's voice soothed in time with his steady strokes along the back of her head and neck. Then along her shoulders. One hand on each side, he patted and braced her in case she fell forward again. "Keep breathing."

She drew in air tinged with the scent of his soap and her magnolia trees outside. Long after her stomach settled, she stared at Vic's work boots and feared what she would find if she looked up. Would he suspect? Hopefully he didn't know anything about pregnant women.

What a stupid thought. Of course he did. His ex-wife had been pregnant once.

Slowly, Claire straightened, but she found nothing more than concern on his face. The wisteria plants on her wallpaper stayed blessedly still, although her face in the armoire mirror matched the leaves on the vines.

Vic kept both hands on her shoulders. She couldn't seem to scavenge the words to tell him she no longer needed his support.

For just one weak moment, she let herself forget her fears about being a good mother, about holding strong against all the people clamoring to take her house away. Forget that even if she could stay in his arms, Vic had been burned in the past, too. Forget everything but the wonderful deep blue of his eyes as he searched her face.

Staccato footsteps sounded from the hall.

Vic dropped his hands in a flash and stepped back. He scooped her notepad off the floor and plopped it on her bedside table by a colored-glass bowl of rocks.

Inching off the bed, Claire grabbed the bedpost for support. She knew full well her shaky knees had more to do with Vic than his baby.

Starr blasted through the door, water glass, cloth, and thermometer in hand. "Oh good, you're awake." Her spiky heels clicked across the waxed wood floors. "Sorry it took me so long, but I couldn't find the thermometer. And oh, uh, your medicine cabinet's not quite as organized anymore." She gasped for breath, setting everything on the bedside table. "You scared the spit out of me."

"Sorry about that." She reached for the glass and dutifully swallowed down two sips before setting it by her notepad and decorative rocks.

"And well you should be." Her foster sister shoved her down onto the bed with a strength that would have surprised most people.

But not Claire. She knew her fireball sister better than that. Nobody tangled with Starr. Well, not anyone with sense. A cold cloth slapped across her forehead.

Vic leaned against the wall next to her

armoire. "She hasn't eaten today. Something about being too busy."

Claire shot him a *you traitor* look, before smiling at her sister. "No need to take my temperature. I just need to grab a quick bite and I'll be fine."

Her nausea usually didn't last past the afternoon. She'd tried to arrange her schedule for later shifts so she had mornings to lie in, but preparations for the baby shower tonight had skewed her schedule.

"Yeah, right." Leaning, Starr creaked open the trunk at the foot of the bed and whipped out an extra pillow. She thunked it at the end of the mattress. "You're going to put your feet up and sleep. I'll bring you a sandwich in a minute."

"But the—"

"Baby shower. I own a third of this place, you know. I can hostess an event on my own just like you do."

But the cooking wasn't Starr's area of expertise. She managed the bar as well as handling the artsy side of decor and the gift shop, while accounting major Ashley had taken over the books.

Still, they did all help out with waitressing in a pinch.

Starr bustled to the window and closed the blinds. She left a few inches free at the bottom for the wind to slant through since the AC barely worked. "Ashley will be here in a few minutes. She and I can pull the rest together before tonight, and still watch over the restaurant."

"But you don't know what I've—"

"Good Lord, girl." Starr swished to the door and flicked on the ceiling fan. "You've been making detailed lists for as long as I can remember. I'm sure you've got one around here somewhere. Just give it to me and I'll take things from there."

Claire patted her right apron pocket. Empty. But she always kept it there. Of course, she'd been distracted lately. She fished inside her left.

Empty as well. Oh yeah, it had fallen out. "I know the last-minute list is here some—"

Vic slid the pad off her bedside table. "Is this it?"

He paused mid-reach, frowning. His eyes locked on the top sheet of paper. Claire followed his gaze… right…down…to his lunch selection bordered with baby bottles. Then he looked up. At her.

At her stomach.

His rugged face blanched as white as her bleached lace curtains gusting in the window. *He knew.* She didn't even have to wonder. Her throat closed.

His paleness quickly shifted to something darker. Thank heavens her sister stood behind him. Anger stamped itself across his normally easygoing face and in his beautiful eyes. Who knew blue could turn to black?

She understood he had every right to be angry with her for not telling him sooner, but that didn't stop the swell of disappointment. Silently, Vic dropped the pad on the bed and scratched a hand along his chest, right over his heart.

Claire yanked the little notebook up and ripped the top page off before passing the rest to Starr. "Here, this has a list of the last-minute errands."

At least Starr seemed oblivious as she babbled nonstop. "Where did you put the guest list? I've already made the centerpieces and party favors. Does Ashley have the games, or did she already drop them off?"

Claire answered automatically, unable to drag her eyes from Vic's face as it blanked of all expression. "On the computer. In the Shower section, folder marked Rena Price. And yes, Ashley has the games."

Starr flipped through the notes. "What about the menu listed on your notepad? Where do I find everything?"

The notepaper crumpled in her fist. "Check

the freezer, second from the top shelf, for the things I baked ahead and froze. The rest is in the pantry."

"Labeled, I assume."

"Of course." Claire forced herself to swallow past the wad of regret in her throat. "I'm sorry," she said, more to Vic than her sister.

Starr tossed a lightweight quilt over Claire's legs. "Don't apologize, hon. You pull more than your share living here while I hide out in the carriage house. I'll be back in a second with a sandwich."

Her foster sister stepped away to hook arms with Vic and began inching him out of her room with a knowing look that didn't bode well for secrecy. "Thanks again for the muscle help."

"Anytime." Vic nodded. "Good-bye, Claire."

His mouth might have said good-bye, but his determined eyes said clearly they'd be talking soon.

* * *

She hadn't seen the last of him, Vic vowed.

Frustration fueled his feet as he charged down the front steps of the restaurant, across her yard toward the marina. He strode past the Beach-combers' white wooden sign, seashells piled around the base in place of landscaping rocks. His gaze locked on home, his Catalina sailboat. His head still buzzed with numbing realization like the bees zipping through the blooming azalea bushes.

Claire was pregnant.

Vic slapped a mosquito snacking on his neck, the sting nowhere near as sharp as the one inside him. She'd lied. Lied in that message, and again every day after with her continued silence.

He'd been an idiot, especially today, in missing the signs. He'd attributed the fainting spell to exhaustion. When her face flooded with that telling shade of green, a flipping bullhorn had sounded in his head. But he'd ignored it even though he'd seen that nauseated hue on Sonya's face a time or two—or five.

Then he'd seen the baby bottle border on Claire's pad, followed by her guilty blush, and he couldn't ignore the obvious any longer.

She was pregnant. He was going to be a father again, and the kid *was* his. He'd watched Claire's house from the deck of his boat often enough to know she wasn't dating anyone else.

Still, she'd known about the pregnancy for months and hadn't said a word to him.

Vic thudded down the dock, water below him slapping the posts and the hulls of everything from ski boats to yachts. He closed in on his forty-two-footer, the *Dakota-Rat*. He'd wanted to name her Emma, but that seemed morbid at a time he'd vowed to get his act together.

Or so he'd thought.

He leaped from the dock to the bow. He should head inside and…what?

His feet stalled. Maybe he deserved her

silence after the pathetic assurance he'd scrounged up during their broken-condom incident. Of course none of that mattered now if there was a child to consider.

A child.

Vic stopped by the wheel and grabbed the rail for support. His hand slid up to scratch his chest over his thudding pulse. He knew he wouldn't be able to keep himself from loving this kid. But man, he was scared. Flat-out terrified of placing his heart in chubby little hands again.

Apparently, the choice had been taken away from him.

Resting his elbows on the warm metal railing, he gazed across the water at Claire's white clapboard house. The wraparound porch with hanging ferns swaying in the wind offered a welcoming vision he knew wasn't meant for him.

He would leave her alone for her much-needed nap and the shower party thing. But before morning, he and Claire would have one very straightforward discussion. He'd had enough of Claire shuffling him aside.

Even though the thought of marriage knocked his sea legs out from under him, no way would he walk away from his child.

Three

"That makes at least seven children for Rena Price!"

Starr's announcement about broken ribbon superstitions jangled in Claire's ears, the restless nap having done little to settle her nerves. She normally enjoyed baby showers and all their sentimentality, but not tonight.

Although Claire had to admit, her sisters had pulled everything together well while she slept.

They'd closed off the smallest of the three

dining areas, leaving the two other rooms and the back bar open for business. Chairs for the thirty-four guests perched in a semicircle by a banquet table of presents, the buffet lining the back wall. Rena reigned from a mauve wingback chair, the expectant mom absurdly regal in her floppy bonnet concocted with gift ribbons and bows. The woman's third trimester pregnant belly had Claire itching to scratch her own expanding waistline.

Instead she checked out the decorations for the tenth time to make sure every floating candle stayed lit in the crystal bowls. Magnolia and gardenia blooms accented clusters of white, pink and blue balloons. A centerpiece basket overflowed with party favors—horseshoes decorated with raffia and ribbon to hang over doors for good luck.

Superstitious Starr's idea, of course.

The inexpensive decorations scrounged from their yard and estate sales weren't too shabby.

Hopefully word would spread, leading to more bookings for showers and rehearsal dinners— even banquets.

Claire swept a stray hair back behind her ear. If only the mess she'd made of her situation with Vic could be as easily handled.

Not for the first time tonight, her gaze gravitated to the open French doors toward his boat docked in the harbor. Dusk left a hazy glow over the water. Lights lined the marina, Vic's boat glowing inside as well since he lived there.

His hard-muscled body made a towering shadowy outline on the deck, no doubt watching for her guests to leave so he could corner her. He lounged against the rail illuminated by a halogen lamp, slowly drinking from the glass in his hand.

Even from a distance, she knew without question the glass contained her tea. He always purchased a gallon to take with him. He never drank alcohol. Never. She'd asked him why once and he'd said something offhand about always being on call for his four-legged patients. She'd wanted to urge him to share, but he'd nuzzled her neck and...

Well, she'd forgotten about questions as well as stocking up on more condoms. Ones with a current expiration date.

"Okay!" Starr waggled a tiny wicker basket in the air. "Now that we're done with the presents, it's time for one more game. My favorite. Baby-Making Mad Libs."

Claire winced. Could this evening be any more torturous? She glanced out the window at Vic—*waiting*.

The answer remained to be seen.

Starr rained slips of paper into the basket. "I've written down everything Rena said when she opened her gifts. We're each going to read one of the comments out loud to learn what Rena said the night she and her husband made this fourth baby."

The shower guests cheered while Claire pulled a tight smile.

Starr shook the basket, the papers rustling inside. "I'll start." She whipped out a strip. "I've never seen one this color before!"

Squeals filled the room, only to be shushed by people eager for the next.

Shy Ashley swished her heavy hair aside and read softly with a sly grin, "All this for me?"

Ashley passed the basket to pregnant Rena who studied the words and snorted. "You shouldn't have."

Amid chuckles the basket made the rounds.

"We'll get a lot of use from this."

"What a handy little tool."

"I wonder if it will fit."

The list continued with laughs and more than one bawdy comeback until the basket landed in Claire's lap last. She couldn't help but think the thing resembled a snake charmer's container. She inched her hand inside and withdrew words guaranteed to torment her tonight.

"Come on," Starr urged, "you have to play, too."

Claire dutifully read her slip. "Now where should I put this?"

Starr's quirked brow shot her a clear message, *no wonder you sleep alone, hon,* before turning back to the room, playing the role of party planner to perfection.

Claire leaped to her feet. The last thing she needed was for this conversation to lead deeper into the subject of baby making. She'd be blushing with guilt in front of a roomful of witnesses. "There's plenty of food left for seconds. Please, everyone help yourselves while I check on the dinner crowd."

Wandering toward the banquet room into the entry hall, Claire sagged onto one of the small sofas out of the way of supper traffic. The live band out back vibrated through the floorboards. She resisted the urge to straighten stacks of painted T-shirts and handcrafted souvenirs. She really did need to prop up her feet.

The front door stood open, salty breeze filtering through the screen. She loved the ocean scent hanging on late-night humidity, the familiarity of the scenery. Keeping the house was worth every bit of stress from launching this business, worth more than any of those outlandish offers for her haven.

Some things were more valuable than money. Home. Family. Love. After Aunt Libby died, Claire had left her chef's job at a downtown Charleston restaurant, joining forces with Starr and Ashley to renovate the place into a bar and grill.

Her eyes hitched and held on Vic's boat. On Vic. She wouldn't enter some marriage of convenience, no matter what he said.

Four years ago Aunt Libby had been expecting to throw a wedding shower for her—until Ross just up and changed his mind. No deep reason or great betrayal. He'd simply decided he didn't love her after all and told her to keep the ring and enjoy wearing it.

As if. She'd fished the rock from her back drawer a year ago and pawned it to finance a new refrigerator.

In honor of the man with an ice-cold heart.

Claire shook off memories of the past. She rarely even thought about Ross anymore. But the failure dogged her now as she wondered how she would handle her discussion with Vic and how she could trust anything that came out of his beautifully sculpted mouth.

She watched him watching her from a distance—and there was no question but that he could see her. Vic lifted his glass in toast to her. She might be confused about a lot of things, but one thing was certain.

She preferred the cool practicality of a new fridge over the heartbreak of a broken engagement any day of the week.

* * *

Vic wasn't leaving until he had straight answers and a solution in place.

Striding past the white wooden sign, he made tracks up the flower-lined walkway at midnight, which reminded him of the first time he'd seen Claire right here, a hot fall Monday afternoon. She'd been painting and perspiring, so naturally sexy he'd almost hit on her then.

Until his Y chromosome radar sensed *it*. The home-and-hearth factor. He'd held strong in keeping his distance for all of what? A few months.

The dining rooms were dark now, although the bar around back still throbbed with the live band's last set. Starr usually managed the bar while Claire oversaw the kitchens. She should be available to talk.

The subject? Marriage.

He sure hadn't expected to go that route again, but he had to offer. He'd fathered this child and he wouldn't let Claire down. No doubt the woman could handle things on her own, but she didn't have to. Claire deserved someone who'd help her, a husband. He wasn't the best man for the job, but he was the one walking up her steps.

"Over here." Claire's voice drifted from the far reaches of the lengthy front porch. The soft creak of a rocking chair moved in synch with the gush and ebb of waves.

Vic pivoted on his boot heels, his eyes adjusting to find her waiting for him past the outdoor tables. She must have come outside during the five minutes it had taken him to sprint off his boat once he'd seen the dining room lights dim and the front porch lamp click off. A low candle flickered on the table beside her, one of those mosquito repellent things, practical and pretty.

Like Claire.

He allowed himself a minute to absorb her peaceful beauty. Her caramel-colored hair fell

loose around her shoulders where he longed to
rest his hands.

*Okay, shut down thoughts that would make
talk all the tougher.* He didn't think well with
his libido engaged. He and Claire had an engagement of another sort to discuss first.

She waved for him to sit in the other rocker,
a glass of his favorite tea ready and waiting. A
peace offering?

Vic claimed the glass but ignored the empty
rocker, too restless to sit. He leaned back
against the porch post and swallowed half the
drink. Crickets and tree frogs blasted a
mocking serenade in the silence between them.
Claire always had been so darned patient. He'd
liked that about her before.

Not now.

He cleared his throat with another gulp and
set his glass on the rail. "So you're definitely
pregnant?"

She nodded, her hair swaying. "Definitely. I

went to a doctor across town so no one here would know."

An awful thought he hadn't considered struck him. "You aren't planning to—"

"No!" Claire straightened, eyes wide. "Absolutely not. I'm keeping this baby. I just don't want anyone in my family to know, not yet anyway."

"Why?"

"Because it will upset them, which is why I hadn't told you."

That helped ease the sting—some—not enough. "Your sisters don't like babies?"

She smiled for the first time, twirling a lock around one finger. "They adore children, and they love babies." Her smile faded. "But they'll worry and hover, and I'm not ready for that."

He forced his tones to stay level in spite of the betrayal roaring through him. "Why did you tell me in that message that you weren't pregnant?"

Remorse flickered in her eyes. Genuine? "I thought I wasn't at first. Sometimes in the early weeks a woman, uh—" she winced "—spots. Do you know what I mean?"

Her words froze him. "Damn straight I know what spotting is. I am a doctor, after all. And you've stayed on your feet in spite of that warning sign?"

"It was one time. Enough to make me think I wasn't pregnant, but an isolated incident. Since there haven't been any recurrences since then, my OB reassures me there's no need to worry anymore."

He searched her face and found too much peace in her expression for her to be lying about the baby's well-being. Some of the tension seeped from his shoulders, although he still intended to have a long discussion with her doctor very soon.

Except hell, Claire could ban him from there, too, if she chose.

He needed some rights. "Well then, you can tell your sisters about the baby after we get back from applying for a license at the courthouse tomorrow."

There. He'd said it. His tie was about to choke him—hey, wait, he didn't wear ties.

"No." Her lone word carried a hefty helping of conviction.

"Come again?"

"No, we're not going to the courthouse."

"Okay, then we'll go talk to your preacher and set something—"

"We're not doing that either because we're not getting married." Her voice stayed steady, but her hands, draped over the armrests, shook.

Vic roped in his frustration. "Run that by me one more time."

"It's honorable of you to want to do the right thing, but there's no need. There's no shotgun at your back. I don't have any brothers or parents to breathe down your neck. I can support my child and myself. You don't have any obligations to either of us."

He watched those trembling hands of hers. The bubbling burn on her elegant finger sent his protective urges into overtime again. "What if I want obligations?"

Claire's brown eyes softened. "I won't keep you from seeing the baby whenever you want. We can even draw up some kind of logical custody arrangement, with visitation rights."

"Whoa. Time out." Vic put his hands together in a T. What happened to him taking care of her? "You can't organize me and my life like your pantry or one of your parties. I don't want some weekend-father gig. I don't want to miss those first steps or words because it's not my weekend to have her."

Her.

Emma.

Vic braced himself against the stab of pain from thinking about his daughter. If he got worked up, he'd scare off Claire. Where she went, his baby went.

He wouldn't lose another child.

Her back might be rigid, but he could soothe her like he did a skittish mare, with patience. "Claire, this isn't about what's right for us, it's about what's right for this baby."

He could see her weakening, then her spine straightened again. "Having parents who're married but don't love each other isn't right either."

Vic agreed with her there. He'd been through a hellish divorce and didn't relish the thought of another.

"I'll do anything to reassure you except lie." He wouldn't hurt her that way, and he knew how lies cut in the end. "If I could love again— and that's a mighty big if—I would choose someone like you."

She was everything he'd ever wanted for himself, everything he'd thought he'd chosen with his ex.

Big-time mistake.

Nope, his judgment in the romance department wasn't the best, but he would be a good dad.

Vic shoved away from the rail and stopped only inches from her. "Give me a chance, Claire, just a chance to show you we can make this work for our kid. We may not have planned this baby but now we're responsible for giving it the best shot we can."

He placed both hands on the arms of her rocker and leaned closer. "Come on. Think about it at least."

Why had he moved so near? Now her lilac perfume was messing with his mind. Not to mention his libido. Memories of their time together flooded over him, not of the bedroom, but before that. He remembered the first time he'd kissed her.

They'd been in her dining room, dimmed light and moonbeams playing across her face, streaming down her neck to caress over the creamy tops of her breasts—like tonight.

Unable to resist any longer, then or now, he leaned, just a few inches and…

He kissed her.

Claire's full lips felt so right softening under his, the attraction between them pounding through him with a steady pulse echoed by the percussion of the band in the distance. At least they had this much going for them. She had to realize this attraction was rare and mighty amazing. Her breathy gasp and gentle sway forward told him she knew it well.

His hands clenched around the rocker's armrests while hers drifted to rest on his chest. Yes. He parted her lips with his tongue, dipped inside for a taste of her. So damn sweet.

And spicy. Her nails dug into his skin as she gripped his shirt front. She tugged him nearer with a kitten whimper that blasted away thoughts and reason until he could only think about sinking deeper into her again.

He allowed one hand to drift up and stroke

her loose hair that had driven him crazy ever since he'd set foot on her porch. So soft, like Claire's smile. One more brush of his mouth over hers and he inched away.

Her eyelids fluttered open. Slowly. And in her gaze he found desire and—

Panic.

His heart thudded. Even as torqued off as he was over her secrecy, the last thing he wanted was to hurt Claire. Backing away, he formed his apology and prepped himself for the worst.

"Okay."

"Okay?" He stopped. His feet grew roots on the planked porch.

"Yes, I'll think about what you said."

A swell of relief started inside him.

"If."

He should have known better. "If what?"

Claire stood, her breasts still rising in an unsteady, rapid pace. "Vic, I need time. I need to sort through what I'm feeling and that's hard enough to do while I'm getting ready for all these catering gigs this week. It's impossible with you…close."

Her chest rose and fell faster, her pupils dilating.

So she was unsettled by the attraction? Not a bad thing in his book. "You've already put me off for over three months. How do I know you aren't just putting me off again?"

Her hands fell to her stomach and damn it, he wanted the right to touch their child, too. Wanted the right to touch Claire.

"Vic, I'm sorry. I know time's running out, and I can't hide my expanding waistline much longer. But this is too important to risk an impulsive, uh, thing, uh, you know. Marriage," she spit out the word like a bad bite of apple. "I'm really overwhelmed with work right now. My biggest catering event ever—a rehearsal party that could bring in tons more business—is slated for this Friday. We can talk more after that."

They would *talk* about it? That was her *yes?*

She couldn't even call marriage to him more than a *thing*. Not a resounding endorsement for hope.

Yet at least she'd left a crack in the door. He intended to jam his foot right in that opening so she couldn't slam the door in his face again. Vic shoved aside lingering doubts from his first fiasco—uh, marriage—and set his course. He planted his boot heels on the porch, intent on hashing this out now.

Only to be cut short when she swayed.

"Damn it, Claire," he cupped her elbow, "you have to take care of yourself."

"For the baby. I know. It's just been a long day." She didn't pull away. Exhaustion?

Or an answering desire?

"I meant for you, too." His thumb stroked along the crook of her arm, a surprise erogenous zone he'd discovered on day two of loving every inch of her voluptuous body.

"Are you sure you're all right?"

She eased her arm from his hold and

cradled it to her swelling waist. "I just need more sleep."

Well, that effectively shut down his arguments for the night. "All right, then. I'll see you inside."

"I can walk by myself." She backed toward the door.

He should let her go. Should. And he would.

Once he saw her safely up the stairs. "If you go by yourself, you'll run into Starr and think of something else you can do out in the bar. I'm sticking by you all the way up to your room."

"The kitchen's closed down even for bar food this time of night. Starr can handle closing fine with the bartender's help—" She stopped short. "Never mind. I'm too tired to argue. You can escort me upstairs, but I won't be pulling you down beside me this time."

Regret pinched. Hard. "I didn't ask."

He backed for her to pass, ready to catch her at a moment's notice. He followed her through the side door, not bothering to keep his eyes off the sweet view since there wasn't anyone to notice or censure. Ambling past her kitchen, he inhaled the scent of baked goods, herbs, flowers…and something else.

His nose twitched, instincts firing to life. "Claire? Do you smell that?"

"Sweet heaven, I smell everything these days, one of the side effects of pregnancy, my doctor says. Every scent like that flower there is doubled…" Her feet slowed, her pale face blanching even whiter. "Vic? Omigod, there's a gas leak."

Gas leak? His instincts burned hotter. The whole darn place could blow at any second. His gaze shot to the fire alarm on the wall. One quick flick of his hand sent the siren blaring.

Without another thought, he scooped Claire into his arms for the second time in one day and hauled butt toward the door. No way in hell was he setting her loose anytime soon.

Four

"**Y**ou can set me down any second now, Vic."

Claire gritted out the request for the third time since he'd dashed from her kitchen with her in his arms. Hot, muscled arms. He cradled her to his yummy chest with her face pressed to his neck scented with aftershave.

She gasped air laden with the thick perfume of azalea bushes and *him* in hopes of breathing away the acrid stench of fumes and fear. Vic kept on holding her close even though they now stood in the middle of evacuated bar patrons. Gawking patrons and neighbors who seemed far more fascinated with the sight of her in Vic's arms than any crisis going on inside Beachcombers.

The fire alarm honked through the night air, her heart nearly as loud as she feared her business— her home—could explode without warning. Thank heavens Vic had reacted so quickly in tripping the alarm and whisking her out.

Help felt nice. Really nice. And sexy. If only she could trust in the draw between them as easily as she trusted in the strength of his arms.

The crowd gathering by the dock parted, Starr sliding through to her side, bar apron over her jean shorts and white Beachcombers T-shirt. "What's going on? Are you okay?"

Her sister screeched to a halt on the grass, eyes going wide as she studied the two of them. Tree frogs croaked along the reedy shore in echo of the distant sirens.

Claire elbowed Vic's stomach until he set

her down, her feet sinking into giving softness of sand and patchy grass. "I'm fine. We smelled a gas leak inside and Vic didn't think I was running fast enough. The fire department should be able to tell us for sure if there's a problem."

His arm stayed around her waist, his fingers grazing the growing curve of her stomach. She inched to the side to adjust his hand to the small of her back.

Her sister's quirked brow broadcast the move had come a second too late. "I thought you'd already left."

His hand didn't budge from its proprietary spot. "I came back."

"You sure did."

The increasing squeal of sirens stalled any further conversation, thank goodness, because she so didn't have the energy to dodge her pushy sister now. They all had far larger concerns anyway.

An hour later, Claire watched the last of the customers drive away along with the fire officials who'd declared that yes, there was a gas leak in her kitchen. While they thought they'd plugged the problem, she needed to get a more thorough once-over from the gas company tomorrow before she could open for business again.

Argh.

Of course the safety of her patrons must come first. Still, if this had to happen, why couldn't it have been on a Sunday night since Monday was a regularly closed day? And now her sister's eyes were narrowing in her direction again, Vic never more than two steps away since he'd hauled her from the restaurant.

Even the nosy marina owner, Ronnie Calhoun, was checking them out from a hundred yards away, looking a little more outrageous than usual with his captain's hat at a jaunty angle.

Enough already. She refused for her or her baby to be gossip fodder. Her private life was her own.

Claire stepped to the side, shifting her attention—and hopefully Starr's—back to the restaurant. "What is up with everything lately? I mean *sheesh,* leaky roof, rotting porch, broken water pipe and now this."

Starr shrugged. "The cost of doing business in an old house, I guess."

"We'll have to stay closed on Sunday, our biggest lunch day with the after-church crowd, plus rescheduling a baby shower into an already packed week."

If they could have had the party on Monday night... But the mom-to-be had been in the crowd tonight and already vetoed Monday in favor of the next week so they would have time to inform everyone. So much pre-prepared food wasted since it wouldn't last until her next party scheduled for Wednesday. More money lost. At least she could freeze the unfrosted layers of cake.

Vic stepped closer, his heat warming her back.

"Looks as if you're getting a couple of days off to rest up after all."

Rest? How could she relax knowing he was so close and the attraction between them hadn't lessened in the least. Her life was careening out of control and the overprotective glint in Vic's eyes had her itchy for space. "Seems you're right. I really should go to bed."

Starr's eyes twinkled with a wickedness that had landed her in the principal's office on a regular basis. "Since you can't go back inside until the place has been cleared, where will you sleep tonight?"

Vic hoped *somebody* had slept last night, because thoughts of what could have happened to Claire if that gas leak hadn't been detected…

He slid farther underneath Claire's porch to check the support beams, cold dirt beneath him doing little to cool his simmering anger. From the second Starr had begun listing all those "accidents," alarms blared in his head as loudly as the one calling for the fire department. What bogus BS—a loose gas nozzle to the stove. *Loosened,* more like it, because meticulous Claire would never miss a detail in her kitchen.

Beyond that, he understood about historic homes and even still the repair list was lengthening too fast for his peace of mind. As best he could tell, there was no reason for this deck to have given way. Although the lone stray board in the dirt with saw marks in the wood set off alarms in his head. Aunt Libby may have been short of cash, but she'd kept the place in good shape for a building a couple of centuries old.

Claire and her sisters truly were sitting on a gold mine here, property value wise. They could sell it to any number of people for a comfortable nest egg rather than grinding themselves into the ground.

A very comfortable nest egg.

However, he understood well the relentless need to hold on to a family house. He'd worked his butt off to save the debt-riddled veterinary practice he'd inherited from his father, and yeah, he could have made it work over time.

But he'd also learned that living life was more important than holding on to the past.

Once he'd come to that realization, he'd sold off his family home and vet practice to hang out with the living. His sister. His niece. His new brother-in-law. He hoped to persuade his only other remaining relative, his cousin Seth, to join them all soon in this fresh start.

Now he had his family around him, a great job in a practice with other vets to take turns on call, and in a surprise by-product that really didn't mean jack to him, he was making triple the income. Not to mention, his boat was a lot easier to keep clean than his rambling house full of painful memories.

Emma's first steps in the kitchen.

Building snowmen by the barn.

Pedaling her trike down a dirt road.

God, when would it stop hurting to think about her?

Of course, Claire had good memories here, and he needed to make sure that stubborn woman didn't risk her health or safety in keeping them. He'd checked everything he could on the outside, and would make a once-over of the inside after the gas company declared the place okay to enter. For now there were no potential problems he could detect, beyond checking out the saw marks on that stray board.

Sliding out from under the house, Vic came face-to-face with pretty feet in orange flip-flops with tiny shells glued on. Tangerine-colored toenails matched, with a Claire perfection to detail that totally turned him on with the irresistible urge to make her messy.

He wrapped his hand low on her leg, gliding his thumb over her ankle, enjoying the view of Claire's pretty feet on the rock bed surrounding an azalea bush. Hmm…maybe he could hang out down here for a while longer.

She frowned at him, a glass of ice water cupped in her hands. "What are you doing?"

"Just checking out your porch." And checking out her cute ankles as well since her shorts showed them off so conveniently. The view stayed just as fine moving up, her full breasts pressed against her loose T-shirt.

"May I ask why?" She sank down beside him.

Vic sat up, elbow on his knee. "Your sister mentioned you've had more than a few accidents around here lately, so I thought I would give the place a once-over."

He could see the pride starching up her spine to tighten her lips. He wanted to press, but he was learning patience worked better with Claire. Besides, looking at her wasn't any great hardship, sun glinting on the golden streaks through her loose hair.

She glanced at the porch then back at him again. "Thank you for your help."

Had practicality or good manners won? Either way, he would accept his victory. "Have you considered hiring someone to do a whole home inspection?"

"I appreciate your suggestion." Starch alert.

"If you're strapped for cash I can—"

"I'm not your responsibility." She plucked wilted petals from the azalea bush, pitched them under the steps to mulch and searched for more dying flowers to prune away.

"I won't argue that point with you—" since he had a feeling he would lose serious ground "—but you also can't argue that where you go, my kid goes. So if it makes you feel less obligated, tell yourself I'm doing this for the baby."

"I'm sorry for sounding like such an ingrate." She passed him a live bloom. "Peace offering?"

A flower *from* a woman? He should be sending them to her by the dozens. Of course, Claire had turned his world upside down from the start.

He took the pink blossom from between her fingers. "We're both on edge."

"What could I do for you?"

She stretched her legs in front of her, T-shirt resting against the bump of her stomach with a reminder of how little time he had left to be patient. Noise from boat motors carried on the wind along with marina guests shouting greetings to one another. Normal life, but a whole universe away when all he could think about was the woman in front of him.

"Vic?"

"Pardon?"

"We're both on edge, like you said." She waved toward the porch of vacant tables and empty rockers. "And you're digging in to help me. What could I do to help you?"

"Marry me."

Laughing, she pitched a fistful of dead azalea blossoms at his chest. "Other than that."

"Can't blame a guy for trying." This woman needed his help taking care of herself whether she wanted to acknowledge the fact or not. He would simply have to figure out a way around her objections. "You have two days off. Spend them with me."

"Yeah, right. That's how we got into this position."

He could think of a few positions he would like to get into with her right now. "We were friends once, don'tcha know. Why not hang out like we used to, settle in, see what it would be like to hang out together long-term?"

"Can you truly say you want to get married again?"

Damn. She'd cut right to the chase.

He hesitated a second too long.

"That's what I thought." She rested a hand on his arm, such a simple touch but so much like their old friendship days he swallowed hard. "Truth be told, I've never had a man in my life who didn't eventually let me down. Trusting you to be my friend is one thing. Trusting you with my heart and my child, is another thing altogether."

"Whoa. Time out." He put his hands together in a T. "Let's back this up. I would be an idiot if I didn't have reservations about marriage. I've got a mighty big screwup in my past. The last thing I want is another woman crying over divorce papers with my name on them."

Straightening, Claire crossed her legs, picking at the grass by her feet, plucking out a small rock and studying it with over-concentration. "I thought she asked for the divorce."

"She did, and she was right." His ex-wife hadn't been able to forgive him for Emma's death, for not protecting the perfect life they'd built as a family. Sonya had said every time she looked at him she thought of their daughter drowning. Hell, he understood because there were still days he couldn't look in the mirror. "It wasn't easy on either of us to walk away. Even a bad marriage shouldn't be painless to end, because commitment is important. Do you understand what I'm saying? I know this has all happened fast, but I want you to understand I *am* taking every word I say seriously."

"Wow," she whispered, staring at him, her little rock clutched in her fist.

"Wow? That's it? I pour out my freaking heart to you and all you can say is 'wow'?"

"You should talk like that more often." She plunked the stone in her pocket and dusted dirt from his T-shirt, taking her sweet time about performing the seemingly "helpful" task. "You're good at it."

"Then let's spend more time together so we can talk and become comfortable around each other for *our* child. I know you said you would think about my proposal, but while I'm waiting for your answer, I need some reassurance I'll be a part of this baby's life."

A part of her life.

Her dusting hand slowed to rest over his thumping heart. "I have work, calls, rescheduling, plenty to keep me busy today."

To make her understand, he would have to go places in his head he preferred to leave back in North Dakota, but the stakes were too high. "I've already lost one child."

He couldn't push the rest of the words up his closing throat, even to win her over. Losing a kid...there was nothing worse than that hell.

Her fingers fisted in his T-shirt, tears glinting in her eyes. "I have a doctor's appointment Monday morning. Would you like to come along?"

Coughing, he cleared his throat and scavenged half a smile. "That's a no-brainer."

She rubbed over his heart once, just once, but her empathy heated through thin cotton. "We'll need to leave at eight."

He ignored the tightness in his chest and pressed ahead for what he knew needed to happen. "And you'll go sailing with me today. Your sisters can meet with the gas company's inspector, and given that you passed out yesterday, I'm sure they'll be relieved you're finally taking care of yourself."

"You want to spend today with me?"

Hadn't he been saying just that for the past ten minutes? For Pete's sake, he thought she'd said he was good at talking. Actually he wanted to recline her back on the grass and kiss her but not while the gossipy marina owner stared with unabashed interest toward the two of them. Ronnie Calhoun would be spreading the details to his sailing buddies by sundown.

They needed privacy. "Yes, I want to hang out with you on my boat today."

"Then ask me."

Exasperation kicked around in his gut. "I just did."

"No, you didn't. You *told* me. A hint for you, big fella—" she paused to tap his mouth "—*asking* works better with me."

Duh. With his fortieth birthday staring him in the face, he should have a better handle on women.

Except this woman was different from any other he'd met, a notion he didn't want to sift around overlong. "Will you go sailing with me today? Let me talk your ear off and pamper you silly because no one else does. And hey, call me a knuckle-dragger, but you're carrying my child, which means I want to do something for you. Wait. Scratch that *want* word. I *need* to do something, be active."

Her hand glided up to cup his face. "You're a very charming knuckle-dragger."

"So that's a yes."

"Are you asking or telling?"

"I stand corrected." He pressed a kiss into her palm. "Is that a yes?"

"Ah, so the charming knuckle-dragger is a quick study."

"I'm trying." Trying his butt off, for more than just them and the baby. He intended to stick close until he figured out if someone was sabotaging her house.

"Yes, I'll spend the afternoon with you." Her hand dropped from his face as she stood. "As for tomorrow, we'll see how today goes."

Then he would just have to make their boating an outing to remember.

She couldn't believe she'd agreed to spend the whole afternoon with Vic.

Perched on the nose of his sailboat, Claire tipped her face and let the sun soak through the wispy fabric of her cover-up. A perfect spring day, not too hot and not too chilly. She wanted the rays on her skin, but she only had her bikini and showing her swelling body to Vic…

Well, she didn't look the same as she had

when they'd crawled into his smaller boat nearly four months ago.

She really did need to invest in some maternity clothes, such as a swimsuit. It wasn't like she'd expected to be pregnant this summer and heaven knows, time for shopping was next to nil. Technically her bikini still fit, even if it was a little snug on top. The second she'd caught a glimpse of herself in the long mirror, she'd started to change, then Vic had arrived and Starr was hollering for her. So she'd grabbed her cover-up and…here she was.

The open water was amazing, soothing, relaxing. He'd been right to bring her. Since even considering proposals and forever made her queasy, she would think about how hot Vic looked in his swim trunks, standing at the edge of the boat, casting his fishing rod. Deep-sea fly-fishing, he'd told her. A highly specialized form that apparently required tons of patience. She usually purchased the fish for her restaurant from Ronnie Calhoun at the marina, but maybe she and Vic could share that king mackerel he'd already caught today, grilled for a romantic dinner where they didn't talk about forever.

Angling back on her elbows, she watched him finesse the line endlessly, wordlessly. In blue-and-white swim trunks, there was still so much of him to fill her eyes. Long legs flexed, muscles bulging, dusted with hair bleached blond from so many hours in the sun and glistening with droplets from the ocean spray.

And his chest, pecs and a six-pack. Whoa, baby. His job with large farm animals required strength, and it showed in the rippling cut of his honed body that housed a doctorate mind.

Brains and brawn, a definite turn-on.

So why not take a chance? Approach this like a serious dating relationship. Once the baby arrived, she wouldn't have the luxury of taking things a day at a time. Her child would need constancy from the get-go—no inviting Vic into her personal life then booting him out.

She should make the most of right now to figure out how they would progress. "How does a guy go from the North Dakota plains to living on the water?"

"North Dakota has water and great fishing." He set his rod into a metal brace holder and stepped over to check the autopilot on the wheel, his shadow stretching across her.

On top of her body.

Where was her drink, because her mouth had dried right up? "I thought you wanted us to get closer, and we can only do that if we talk to each other."

He glanced back at her, wind fingering through his short hair. Lucky wind.

"There was nothing left for me in North Dakota once my sister decided to pack up and move here to be with Bo. The house was empty, quiet. I found myself reaching for a bottle a little too often and decided to take control of my life."

"So you simply sold everything and moved here."

"Pretty much." He settled beside her on the front of the boat, his leg pressed against hers. Accidentally?

Regardless, she couldn't bring herself to move away even as she asked the question clenching her stomach. "And the bottle? Did you leave that in North Dakota, too?"

"I go to Alcoholics Anonymous meetings here in Charleston." He glanced over at her, blue eyes serious, deep as the water stretching ahead of them. Mesmerizingly beautiful. "I may be shooting myself in the foot by telling you that, but I figure it's worse if you find out later."

Now she understood why he only ordered iced tea. A fissure of unease slithered up her spine. "Do you have a drinking problem?"

"I was afraid I was developing one so I hooked up with an AA chapter. A few meetings in, I realized I had something to offer other people who'd lost someone. Helping somebody else helped me a lot more than anything else I'd tried."

As much as his past daunted her, she also couldn't ignore the proactive way he'd gone about addressing things. She'd seen so many people tromp through her mother's life, oblivious to the pain they caused others with their vices. Some of her temporary foster sisters had been substance abusers in denial and resistant to offers of help.

She'd been watching Vic's strength for months without even knowing the half of it. His will ran deeper than she could have imagined.

"What was her name? Your daughter, I mean."

"Emma." He turned back to look at the water.

Dangerous territory, but so essential to who he was. If they were going to get to know each other… "Is it okay if I ask about her?"

Why had she never thought to ask before, when they'd been friends? Instead, she'd relied on snippets of gossip. She'd told herself that conversations about favorite books, recent movies, renovations and even politics fostered a deep friendship. Yet she'd never heard his daughter's name or what story he read to her at night.

Had she subconsciously been dodging deeper waters and the risks of a real relationship?

"You have a right to ask that and more." He stayed silent for three slaps of the hull against the waves before continuing, "Actually, I should talk about her more. She deserves to be remembered. Most folks tiptoe around asking about her for fear it'll send me over the edge."

"Will it?"

"To be fair, there was a time that was true. Now, sure, it still hurts to think about her, but the really bad times are fewer and further between, mostly around big events. Holidays." He swallowed. "Her birthday."

"When was her birthday?" she asked, even as she already realized the answer.

"The night I showed up on your doorstep at ten o'clock with the lame excuse of being out of tea."

She heard what he'd left unsaid, that he'd been craving a drink. The fact that he'd chosen to come to her instead of even his family touched something deep inside her.

Claire slid her hand in his and his fingers folded over hers in a warm, strong grip. "Tell me about her."

"Emma had blond hair, looked a lot like my niece, although they were polar opposites personality-wise. Emma was shy. She hung pretty close to me, even went out on calls with me and told people she would be a doggy doctor when she grew up."

The bittersweetly beautiful image painted itself so vividly across her mind Claire squeezed his hand.

He stood, crossed to a storage nook and

pulled out his wallet, flipping it open to a photo, one of those stock department store studio types. A round-faced little girl, around four, perched on a white wicker chair with a stuffed toy horse cradled to her chest.

His gaze stayed fixed on the picture. "This photo was taken a month before she died. Five years ago."

Staring into those serious little eyes, she could see hints of what her own child would look like. Beyond that she was seeing her baby's sister, and that linked her to the poor dead girl with a protective squeeze of her heart so fierce she almost whimpered.

She traced a finger over the plastic covering, along tiny features that would never reach maturity. "It must have been tough for you at first, being around your niece, Kirstie's her name, right?"

Would Vic think of Emma every time he saw their child?

"At first." Easing the wallet from her hands, he folded it closed again. "But Kirstie's her own person and deserves to be loved for the great kid she is, not as a substitute. Hell, Emma deserves better, too. She's not replaceable. No person is."

Oh, man. She was in serious trouble here from a charm as thick as those muscles. "You're a good man."

"I'm just a man dealing with things as best I can." His thumb worked back and forth over the leather wallet. "I know it's early yet, but have you thought about names?"

"A little. I figured we could each choose one and put the two together." Discussing it all seemed so surreal her skin tingled and heated more from emotion than the piercing sun overhead. "I would like Elizabeth—Libby— for a girl. What goes well with Libby?"

"I'll think on it." He tucked the wallet back into the storage nook.

"And for a boy? Do you want a junior?"

"Junior only works if we have the same last name," he pointed out with a quirked eyebrow.

She couldn't stop a twinge of sympathy. She would hate having such limited control over her child's life, having to ask for everything. "The baby can have your last name even if I don't."

"I'm an old-fashioned guy."

That sympathy helped her be fair, but it wouldn't nudge her into caving when it came to the two of them. "You mean the old-fashioned sort who believes people should marry for love?"

Silence stretched through four slaps of the waves against the hull. "Who's to say we won't love each other with time?"

Her stomach flipped, then settled. He was only trying to maneuver her. How many times over the months had he said he wanted nothing to do with serious relationships after the way his marriage had fallen apart?

"We had great sex, Vic." Amazing sex. "It's not the same thing."

He grinned. "It's not a bad thing."

He had a point, one her body wanted so much to revisit for this magical afternoon under the sun. Right now she couldn't think of a reason why they couldn't have that.

Decision made, she swayed toward him.

Five

Seeing Claire sway toward him shot a bolt of desire straight to his groin, hotter than the sun reflecting off the glassy ocean. It had been a long three-and-a-half months without her.

Vic palmed her back and that's all it took before they were kissing and he wasn't sure who'd moved the farthest, but her soft body was against him. He took her even softer lips as his leg hooked over hers along the boat deck. The skin-to-skin contact of their scantily clad bodies short-circuited his brain. So easily he could tunnel under that whispery thin cover-up of hers, sweep away her bathing suit, lower his swim trunks and be inside her moist heat. No worries about birth control, just sun- and passion-warmed flesh meeting flesh.

Her fingers crawled up his back, clinging to his shoulders with a whimper sigh breathing her consent into his mouth. Into him.

He could taste the lemon from her water on her tongue, sweet and tart at the same time, much like Claire. The softness of her lips, her body, made him ache to stretch over her.

He wanted her, now, this chance at a connection and a means of strengthening the ties between them if only on a physical level….

But he couldn't. Not yet. "I don't want to hurt the baby."

"The doctor said I'm fine, the baby's fine, and doing *this* is totally fine." She dipped her hand into his swim trunks, gliding her fingers down, down…

He forgot how to breathe. "What about the spotting and your fainting?"

"I'm okay." She stroked, caressing base to tip, her thumb grazing over—

He clamped a hand around her wrist. "Last time I checked, they don't let morons graduate from veterinary school."

Frustration creased her serious forehead. "Do you think I would do anything to risk harming my baby?"

That stalled him for a second because bottom line he knew she would be a good mother from day one. Still, he would feel like a better father if he talked to her doctor first. "You're exhausted and I'm concerned about you."

"I am relaxed…for me."

She eased her arm from his grip and plopped back on her butt with a pout—no damn kidding, a childish pout on her dignified face that totally charmed him. Her disappointment stroked his ego as much as her hand had…

well…he needed to keep his thoughts well off that subject for now.

Her eyes lit with a calculated mischief that set off alarms in his brain a second before she rested her palms flat on his thighs like branding irons through his swim trunks. "Wanting you as much as I do right now definitely has me tense."

Her hands inched upward.

She had a point.

And just that fast, he saw a way around the problem. "I'm holding firm to my no-sex stand, but you're right that I can't send you home this uptight, and I've made it my mission today to help you relax."

Her eyes went wary. "Are you going to work some horse-whisperer magic on me?"

He winked. "Believe me, you don't look anything like a horse."

"Thanks, I think."

"First, you need to soak up some sun."

"I am." She hugged her knees, filmy cover-up draping almost to her ankles.

Had she intended for them to have sex with her cover-up on, for Pete's sake? "You have a bathing suit under there, right?"

A rhetorical question since the hints of skin and bikini fabric just barely visible had been driving him crazy all day. He tugged the hem, bunching fabric in his hands as he worked his way up.

"Uh-huh, but—" The rest of her words were swallowed in her cover-up as he hitched it over her head to reveal her two-piece.

Whoa.

Just…whoa.

He couldn't tear his gaze away from the lush beauty in front of him. Her full breasts mounded gently from the floral cups of her top. Her bathing suit bottom tucked just under the unmistakable curve of her stomach. There was something so fundamentally sexy about the earthy appeal of her pregnancy out there in her bikini.

A primal rush pulsed through him. His child. His woman. And if she heard his thoughts, she would almost certainly topple him over backward into the ocean, which couldn't even come close to cooling the heat searing through his veins.

She fidgeted, her hand inching toward her cover-up hanging from his grip.

Ah, hell. He needed to get his head out of his libido long enough to pay more attention to her needs, one of which appeared to be a misplaced sense of embarrassment.

He pitched the cover-up behind him, wanted to toss it overboard. "You're so incredibly sexy it's all I can do to keep my feet under me."

A blush tinged her cheeks a pretty pink that had nothing to do with exposure to the sun. "Thank you."

"I only speak the truth." He spread a fluffy beach towel. "And it's the truth when I say you need to rest. Stretch out, snooze if you'd like. You know you're sleepy, just try and deny it. If you'd like, I'll even phrase it all as a question." She scrunched her nose. "I'll let it slide—this time—because I really am sleepy and the sexy comment earned you some brownie points."

"Just telling the God's honest truth."

He remembered well how often Sonya napped, and while he didn't want to think about his ex, he was also grateful for the pregnancy knowledge he brought into the situation. He needed any edge he could get around Claire.

She eyed the towel with obvious longing. "I'll fry like a lobster."

Vaulting over to the storage nook, he scooped up a bottle of sunscreen from beside his wallet. "SPF 45. You can sleep for at least an hour without a worry."

She extended a hand and he pulled back the lotion. "Uh-uh, lady. I get that pleasure. This nap starts with a massage."

A seductress smile curved her lips. "You really think we can touch without making love?"

"Do you really think anything's going to happen out here in the open?" Still, she eyed him suspiciously—smart woman—so he continued, "I guess there's only one way to find out. Now lie back and close your eyes."

She reclined onto her elbows but kept her eyes open, tracking his every move. He filled his palm with cocoa butter sunscreen and rubbed his hands together. Anticipation stalled his breath halfway up his throat. The thought of touching her skin again…

"Close them," he demanded.

Her lashes fluttered shut and now that she couldn't see him he allowed himself a second, fuller look at her tempting body. She could have been a fertility goddess or one of those cover models exposing her bare belly for the world in a proud display of her femininity.

Long, creamy legs with the sweetest dimples

on either side of her knees reminded him of how well they locked around his waist, heels digging into his butt as she urged him deeper. Now probably wasn't a good time to remember how the slightest touch to the inside of her knees would stir a moan from her. One of her many erogenous zones he'd had the pleasure of discovering during their long weekend together. Up his eyes roved, plotting the path of his hands over her stomach, to the fullness of her breasts.

Massaging her to completion while keeping his own swimsuit in place would be torturous. Of course, pleasuring her would pleasure him very much.

Waiting with her eyes closed for Vic to touch her, Claire struggled not to fidget or otherwise ruin the moment giving away her nervousness, and an anticipation she hadn't felt in…well…

Since they'd made love nearly four months ago.

She didn't pass over control often, but this seemed such a harmless little thing, and heaven help her, she wanted his hands on her body again, even if just to smooth on sunscreen.

"Uh, Vic? Are you still there?"

"Very much so," his voice rumbled through her heightened senses. "I'm going to touch your face first, so don't open until I'm done."

Still resting on her elbows, she tipped her face toward him, sun casting an orange glow behind her lids, then darkening as Vic moved closer. His callused fingers slid over her cheeks, up to her temples, massaging as well as spreading the protective lotion with slow deliberation.

Down her neck.

A sigh of longing whispered up her throat. Now he would make his move, and even wanting him, she also longed to continue with this soothing assault on her senses a while longer. His hands lifted away.

Had that whimper really come from her?

She heard the lotion squelch from the bottle and held her breath. Vic gripped her calf, slicking cream over the length of her tired muscles. Her arms gave way beneath her and her spine melted onto the towel, along with the rest of her will.

His strong fingers climbed both legs, over every inch. "We can't have any sunburned patches."

Her nerves were already pretty much scorched.

His hands skimmed upward to the high cut of her bathing suit bottoms, along her exposed hips...

Before hopscotching over to lift one of her hands. Somehow the touch became no less sensual even on her fingers, up her wrist, over her arm and her shoulders down the other arm. He'd covered everywhere except...

His hands splayed over their baby. She forced herself not to tense her mellow muscles, not so difficult since she'd gone boneless somewhere around the time he grazed the inside of her knees. And uh, why hadn't she realized how little her bikini top covered? Or perhaps it seemed to conceal less since her breasts were larger with the pregnancy.

More sensitive, too.

"If you roll over, I'll take care of your back."

Disappointment stung as hard as the needly prickles of desire pulling her nipples painfully tight. She'd thought he planned…

But that wouldn't be fair to him given his vow they wouldn't have sex until she'd seen the doctor. Tomorrow. She just had to wait less than twenty-four hours.

A flipping eternity at the moment.

"Claire? Your back?"

"Oh, uh, I'm afraid I lost the ability to lie on my stomach comfortably about a week ago."

He stretched beside her. "As long as you don't stand up, your back should be fine." He traced the rim of her suit top, just below her aching breasts. "Do you mind if I take this off?"

Sunbathing topless? "I've never…"

"But do you want to?" He traced side to side.

"I thought you said nothing would happen out here in the open."

"Yeah, well, I lied."

She shivered. "Thank goodness."

"There's no one here to see except me and I've already seen everything. So how about giving up that top?"

She dipped her head in the smallest nod.

He slid his hand underneath. She bowed upward to accommodate and next thing she knew, her bikini top swept up and off, air and sun simultaneously cooling and heating her skin. Her nipples puckered, reaching for the heat.

Reaching for Vic.

His mouth closed over her, hot, damp, teasing with a flick of his tongue, his hand cupping her other breast for equal attention. He rolled the beaded hardness between two fingers, plucked, tormented, endlessly…

And then nothing.

His hands left her flaming body.

Her eyes snapped open to find him beside her, breathing raggedly. Magnificently aroused in his swimsuit.

She reached, but he clamped her wrist, stopping her. "Not today, Claire."

"But you said there's no one here. You can't leave us both hurting like this." Her hips rocked against him in time with the give and roll of the boat hull.

"I know. The last thing I want is to hurt you." Vic covered her mouth with his, tongue bold and sweeping. "Trust me."

His fingers sketched over her stomach, lower and into her swimsuit. Her legs fell open and his touch dipped into her dampness and circled. Already so close to the edge, she writhed along the beach towel. The risqué decadence of being outdoors swelled the need faster within her.

Vic tweaked with just the right amount of

pressure he must have remembered from their weekend together and she so didn't want to think of how that had abruptly ended. And who could think now anyway with liquid fire coursing through her veins, sunshine kissing her body as thoroughly as Vic's mouth, endlessly. His fingers pulled the tension tauter… until…

Her cry of completion surged through her like the waves rippling across the water, continuing, the shore and end slipping further away. Pleasure stretching, repeating until finally, she sagged back on the towel, totally and completely sated. She drifted off to sleep, one thought whispering through as teasingly as the wind over her bared skin.

Her doctor visit tomorrow to reassure Vic couldn't come soon enough.

He hadn't expected to return to the OB circuit, yet here he was pulling out of a doc's parking lot with the mother of his child at his side cradling an ultrasound picture.

They couldn't determine the gender, but he'd seen the heart pulsing, tiny arms and legs flailing around in his or her watery haven. Apparently healthy, thank God.

Turning onto the highway, Vic steadied his breathing even though it did nothing to ease the roar in his ears louder than the wind rushing through his open truck windows. This kid was real, with a tiny fist firmly gripping the half a heart he had left. He'd barely survived last time, had in fact decided never to risk a repeat.

But here he was.

Then there was the whole jumbled mess with Claire. He admired her, enjoyed her company— and yeah, her body. But even if he somehow managed to persuade her to marry him, would she be content with only half a heart?

Not that any of this thinking did him a lick of good.

Batten down his defense. Focus on the moment and his kid and the good news that everyone was fine. The doc had been extra cautious because of the spotting, but with Claire entering her second trimester with no further incidents, the doctor assured them all looked well.

She was totally clear to have sex.

He gripped the steering wheel, guiding them onto one of the many bridges linking coastal Charleston and all its barrier islands, church steeples poking at the sky. Water nearly everywhere reminded him of his boating day with Claire and the unfinished promise.

So he would forge ahead with his plan to romance her, because all reservations aside, he was committed to building something with her. Making love with Claire was certainly not a hardship.

They could laze in her bed since yesterday the gas company had declared her house clean of leaks. And beyond that, he should hear soon from the full home inspection company he'd hired. No doubt when she found out that he and Starr had made the decision while Claire napped yesterday, there would be hell to pay, but her safety and the safety of his baby were too important.

During Sonya's pregnancy, she'd landed in the hospital twice for cramping, once when her father had a heart attack and again after too long at a county fair. So you bet, he couldn't escape the need to cosset Claire. Was that so wrong?

He would tell her after he'd heard the inspector's results. Why worry her needlessly with his concerns about the house? And he *would* tell her before getting naked together, and damn, it pinched to think she might boot him out.

His beeper buzzed from his belt.

Claire startled from her dazed staring at the ultrasound printout. "What's that?"

"My pager." He glanced at the LCD screen

and winced. "Looks like lunch will be delayed." As well as sex. "Mrs. Bethea's horse. Do you mind if I take you home and then we meet up around two instead?"

The inspector should be done and gone by now.

"Of course I don't mind." She carefully slid the ultrasound photo back into the protective envelope. "This seems like a good time to start a baby scrapbook while you finish up at Mrs. Bethea's farm."

"Not a farm exactly. She has a horse. A pet horse. When her husband died, she sold off most of the land to support herself, but she kept the homestead and barn. The guy who bought everything else lets her graze Trooper with his herd."

"So the horse is all she has left."

"Pretty much. About twice a month she's convinced Trooper's going to die. I go out there, declare him healthy, and we have a cup of coffee."

"She's lonely."

He shrugged.

"How sad that she has to pay people to visit her."

He stayed quiet.

"She does pay, doesn't she? No? Doesn't your boss have a problem with that— Wait. This is a day off for you. You go out there on your day off?"

Sniffling, she fished through her canvas purse and came back up with a tissue and a tiny stone. What was it with her and the rocks?

"Hell, if I'd known that was all I had to do to win you over, I'd have told you about Mrs. Bethea a long time ago."

"Don't go getting a big head." Tissue a wadded mess, she dabbed and sniffled. "Pregnancy hormones make me cry all the time."

Somehow the normalcy of that reaction made the baby even more real, an inescapable reminder that the stakes were getting higher by the second to persuade her to marry him.

* * *

Surely she was only thinking about engagement rings and wedding bells because of the upcoming rehearsal dinner at Beachcombers on Friday. Not because of the ultrasound still fresh in her mind or the sweetness of how Vic was dropping everything to tend an old lady's pet horse.

The tempting spicy scent of Vic beside her in the truck didn't help keep up her defenses either. "Do you miss having your own practice, where you can pick and choose how to spend your work hours?"

"Sometimes." His eyes went distant as they exited the highway, then he shrugged it off with a smile. "But buying into a clinic with partners has its upside. I have more free time to romance a certain sexy restaurant owner into my bed again."

"You don't have to romance me." She rolled the tiny blue rock between her fingers, a stone that had caught her eye on her way into the doctor's office and soothed her with its talisman effect for the following two hours before she'd stuffed it into her purse.

"Maybe I'm enjoying myself."

"And we'll both get to enjoy ourselves once you've finished up with Trooper." She reached to scratch a nail lightly along his jaw to his chin. "I'll be waiting for you when you're done."

He dipped his head to nip her finger. "You'll use the time to rest and work on that baby book?"

"I promise not to pick up anything heavier than my cellphone to check on some fresh-catch orders I need to reschedule with the marina owner."

"Work, huh? Your sisters are gonna be torqued if they find you and Ronnie Calhoun scheduling fish deliveries. They're worried about you, which isn't going to get better if you're still overextending yourself."

He knew well what buttons to push. She still

wasn't ready to tell her sisters. The last thing she wanted was to worry her sisters, her best friends. Her only family.

Other than this baby.

And what about Vic? a little voice niggled.

The mid-morning sun glinted off his close-cropped hair, his polo shirt revealing a patch of bronzed neck tempting her to kiss. Sex and friendship. *Was* it enough?

"Claire?" He glanced across the truck bench seat at her. "You're not going to worry your sisters, are you? You have to tell them soon."

"You're playing tough today."

"It's obvious the three of you have a tight bond."

She clenched the rock in her hand, its cool slickness centering her. "We had a lot of foster sisters over the years who came and went, but only the three of us stayed."

Three who were never adopted or sent home.

"What about your foster parents?"

"Just a foster mother, actually. Aunt Libby."

Her grip loosened on the stone. "Her fiancé died in the Korean War and she never married. She was amazing, I mean really amazing—eccentric as all get-out. She inherited the house and pinched pennies to live off family money her whole life. Instead she gave all her time to parenting foster daughters."

"She sounds like an incredible woman."

"I wish everyone had recognized that." They'd been lucky to have her, something she hadn't realized at first as child after child found a home while she stayed. "The neighborhood was kinda miffed for a long time. Well, not everyone, but some of the blue bloods were upset to have problem kids from different backgrounds living close by."

"That really blows," he said simply, with that wonderful Vic-way of empathizing without belaboring the point.

"Yeah, although occasionally, their fears

were well-founded." Her mind winged back to the first time she'd seen someone overdose.

"I'm guessing you weren't involved in one of those occasions."

"You would guess wrong." Even though she'd never done drugs, she'd had her own rebellious moments. She tucked the stone back into her purse to store with her others later.

"You have a wicked side?" Truck idling at a stoplight, he glanced over with a twinkle in his eyes. "Wait, I've already seen that side of you very well."

Awareness prickled along her skin, pulling her breasts tight and hungry for the touch of more than his eyes. If they spoke anymore about yesterday topless under the sun, she would explode before they made it back to privacy.

His hand inched across the seat to her knee,

under the hem to stroke along the sensitive inside of her thigh, into the crook of her knee.

How long until he could take care of that lady's horse?

Next time she finished, she wanted him naked with her. "Hands on the wheel, big fella."

Chuckling, he withdrew his touch from under her dress.

She squeezed her legs together against the uncomfortable urge to straddle his lap. "I had my moments as a teenager. Mrs. Hamilton-Reis, next door, never liked Starr. How can somebody look at a ten-year-old child and decide she's evil?"

"Mrs. Hamilton-Reis? Is her house the one that just went on the market?"

"That's the one." Poor old bat. "She's physically in great shape, but her mind is starting to slip. Her children need the money to take care of her."

"And what does all this have to do with your wicked side?"

"Mrs. Hamilton-Reis had these prize fish."

"I've seen the little garden pond and decorative bridge in her front yard."

The old lady's pride and joy, once upon a time. "One night I snuck out of the window and I put a bunch of mongrel fish from a local pet store into her decorative pond."

"You added fish?"

"Same family of fish—" she'd spent hours at the library studying up "—but not purebred."

Her vet-lover grinned, obviously quick on the uptake. "You tainted her breeding lines, you wicked woman."

"The next generation of fish looked really ugly." Mutts. Like her. "Of course, she blamed Starr, even after I confessed that I did it."

"I can see how she may have drawn that conclusion."

The old lady had carried a grudge for years, lasting through teenage years when Starr and Mrs. Hamilton-Reis's son started climbing out

windows together. "I cleaned her pond, and
Aunt Libby joined me, her jeans rolled up to
the knees. The whole neighborhood gawked
while she waded in alongside me. I realized
then that I hadn't done a thing to avenge Starr.
In fact I'd made everyone resent us and Aunt
Libby even more."

The whole experience had been an eye-
opener. From then on, she'd done her best not
to let Aunt Libby down in any way. She was
still working on that.

Towering historic homes stretched down the
street, gentle harbor waves lapping at the shore
in soothing gushes that had lulled her to sleep
for nearly twenty years. Even old Mrs.
Hamilton-Reis's looming brick house, with its
For Sale sign, had a place in her heart like a
cranky relative. The aging owner pruned her
azaleas with a hacking vengeance and energy
beyond her years.

What would Aunt Libby have thought about the

baby? Would she have wanted her to marry Vic? The woman had been eccentric enough to support her *single* motherhood decision, but she'd also been a real romantic, keeping her fiancé's photo by her bed until the day she died.

"You miss her—Aunt Libby." Vic's statement broke through her musings.

Claire nodded, her throat tight with the scent of azaleas and memories.

"Do you still keep in touch with your biological parents?"

"My mom died of hepatitis when I was nineteen. She never gave up hope of getting me back."

Which meant she could never be adopted. Her feelings for Tina were a mishmash of love and resentment and sympathy. If only emotions could be as carefully organized as her pantry. "I never knew my father." She glanced at Vic with a shrug as they neared the only home she'd ever known. "I was a backseat mistake. Her parents booted her out and the boy—my father—denied I was his."

Vic reached to take her hand, squeezing once. "Our baby will never be made to feel like a mistake."

His voice rang with a surety she soaked up like rays of sun on her skin after a long winter.

"Thank you."

She so didn't want to talk about this anymore. She wanted the forgetfulness his body could bring her. She wanted him to somehow convince her they could be right together. "Let's put heavy talk on hold. Finish up with Mrs. Bethea's horse so we can enjoy an afternoon in my bed, complete with the all clear for nonstop sex."

"I do like that wicked side of yours." He glanced at his watch.

His watch?

"Is there a problem?"

"No. Now should be fine."

"Now?"

Did he have a surprise planned for her at home?

Nerves—and more than a little excitement pattered in her stomach as he turned the corner toward her seaside house.

His frown shifted the excitement to a darker hue. She followed his line of sight to her home. To a big truck parked out front.

A truck with a home inspection company logo on the door.

Now should be fine? Vic had known about the inspector? Why would he keep that a secret?

Regardless, she had the sinking feeling the answer would ruin their afternoon plans.

Six

Vic swallowed back a curse that would only make things worse and stepped out of his truck. He circled around the hood seconds ahead of Claire vaulting off the running board, her lips tight. He should have seen this coming, but he'd planned to ease her into it after the fact, later on his boat or in her house.

Starr stood by the porch, looking back and forth from the two of them. Glitter shook from her hair to sprinkle the porch, probably from whatever arts and crafts project Claire's sister had in the works today. "Did y'all have a nice breakfast out?"

"Great." Claire stopped beside her, the two sisters such a contrast—Claire, smoothly elegant in her simple loose dress and Starr, a barefoot whirlwind in jeans. Yet the bond between them was unmistakable. "Did something else go wrong with the house?"

Starr's gaze snapped right over to Vic. "Um, no. I hired somebody to give the place a once-over."

"Oh. Sorry I jumped to conclusions."

While he appreciated Starr's attempt to deflect the fire, honor dictated he fess up now and try to salvage what he could or Claire would never trust him. "It was my idea. I called a friend, and yes, it's my credit card number on the invoice."

Starr hitched her fists on hips. "Sheesh, Jansen, I offered you an out. But noooo, you have to do the macho thing and get her all riled up." She turned to Claire. "He's a good guy who was worried about us and offered a helpful solution at a time you were too worn out to stay awake for more than five minutes at a stretch. I made an executive decision, so if you're going to be mad, give me at least fifty percent of that anger."

"Thank you, Starr." Claire's lips pursed tighter, which made Vic want to kiss them full again. "But Vic and I need to talk."

"You're such a drama queen." Starr spun away in a flurry of hair showering more glitter onto grass. His only potential ally disappeared around a sprawling magnolia toward her carriage house.

Damn.

He pivoted back to Claire. "I planned to tell you after lunch, before we took things any further."

"And that makes it okay to go behind my back?"

"You didn't mind when I checked under your porch."

"That was doing a friend a favor, like if I'd baked you some muffins. Money is a different matter altogether, and I specifically told you I didn't want you to spend anything on my house."

Pretty much. Hell. He was screwed.

Vic leaned back against an oak tree, lowering his voice so the old lady next door with her killer clippers wouldn't overhear. "Consider the money spent on my kid. Not you. I'm just starting the child support early."

"The prenatal payment plan."

Since she wanted the bald truth, he might as well go for broke. God knows, pampering this woman had sure as hell backfired on him. "I'm concerned that somebody is sabotaging your place to drive you out of business."

"Then you should have told me that right away."

"And you would have let me hire someone to check the place out?" He glanced down at his boots to gather his thoughts, then back up to her angry—and hurt—eyes. "Sonya had a few miscarriage scares when she overtaxed herself or got stressed. I was just trying to look out for your health."

"That's what all this has been about?" Anger and hurt faded until he couldn't read her mood. Dangerous. "Looking out for me?"

He knew a trick question when he heard one. He just wasn't sure what the right answer was. "Uh, no, not exactly."

"Wow, what a resounding affirmation." And just that fast her eyes flooded with tears he knew were hormonal, yet they squeezed his gut all the same. "The romance and attention was about protecting the baby."

Whoa. Hold on just a minute.

"And you." Shoving away from the tree, he gripped her shoulders so small and soft and sexy, and probably as much as he would get to touch today—forever—he didn't salvage this fast. "You have to know you're important to me, too."

Had he really forgotten to tell her that?

"I'm not sure what I know right now except my life has spun out of control so fast." She backed away, from under his hands, toward her house in retreat. "I need time to absorb all these changes."

She wasn't saying no. Good sign. Right?

"I think you should take the time. But who says we have to spend that time apart?" He reached again and squeezed her shoulders in a gentle massage until she teetered toward him. He stepped closer, until the tips of her breasts brushed his chest.

Rustling branches from around the porch startled her back a step and had him reaching for her again in an instinctive need to keep her safe from…what?

The inspector cleared the corner, clipboard in hand as he made his way toward them.

"Since I'm a practical woman, I might as well take the report that's already been completed."

She turned to the uniformed man. "Is my house safe to live in?"

"Yes, ma'am, everythin' appears sound. I'll mail you my detailed inspection notes."

"Excellent, and please include your bill with that." She shot a look back toward Vic then returned her attention to the inspector. "Made out to me."

The inspector, a buddy of his from Alcoholics Anonymous, looked for confirmation, which only served to stir another sigh from Claire.

Vic nodded. "Whatever the lady says."

"Fair enough."

Claire reached for the report. "Thank you for making the trip out on such short notice."

"Not a problem at all, ma'am. I had work out this way doing a home inspection for the folks interested in buyin' the Hamilton-Reis place." He flipped the pages on his clipboard as he backed away. "Y'all have a good day now."

Vic leaned a shoulder against the porch post and

weighed his options. He could see her softening and if he pushed, he could probably persuade her to join him for the afternoon, where they would likely end up naked together.

But did he really want to begin their new start with him pushing? Her silently resenting?

No. Damn. Ouch. "Claire?"

"Yes?"

"Let's put that late lunch on hold. I'm going to head out to Mrs. Bethea's, then catch up on some back issues of *DVM* magazine. You can play with some frosting on a cake or whatever relaxes you."

"I thought we were going to, uh…" Her confused eyes rewarded him and affirmed his decision since she wasn't spitting fire his way anymore.

"Have sex this afternoon?"

She shrugged.

He shoved his hands into the back pockets of his jeans. "That wouldn't be giving you time, would it?"

"You're really telling me you're okay with ending our day now? You don't want to make love with me?"

"I never said that last part." A wry smile hitched through his frustration. "As a matter of fact I'm sure you'll never hear those words come out of my mouth. But it's obvious you have reservations and if we get on my boat or in your bed, we're only going to end up arguing about the inspector or something else. I'd rather end our day like this."

"Like this?"

"This." He leaned to skim his mouth over her, deepen just enough to stir a moan in her chest as her lips parted. He kept his hands jammed in his back pockets, limiting their contact to mouths and tongues and, holy hell, if he kept this up much longer, he wouldn't be able to pull away.

Vic stepped back.

Claire swayed, her eyes still closed. "Vic?"

"We'll talk tomorrow."

Before he could change his mind, he pivoted on his boot heels toward his truck. Thank goodness Starr had agreed to call a guy friend to camp out in her place for a while to offer an extra set of eyes to watch over things until he could rest easier about these "accidents" around the house.

From his boat he could also keep his eyes on the restaurant to watch out for any porch saboteurs. The independent woman personified prickly and in need of space, so very different from emotional Sonya who'd preferred he take care of any problems that arose.

He'd been right not to push Claire. Except damn it all, being right sure hurt at the moment.

Why did winning her way have to hurt so much?

Claire kept her eyes on the front door of her home. As she thudded up the porch steps, Vic's truck engine echoed in her ears like the rumble of distant thunder. She couldn't stop the tears making faster tracks down her face. Hormonal tears, right?

She told herself it was a little thing and he'd only meant to be helpful. Still she couldn't stop the niggling fear that if she ignored the inspector issue, she would lose control. She knew from her mother's example what happened when a woman couldn't manage her own life.

Okay, and her ego stung over the notion that he was only doing this all because of the baby, a totally silly frustration since she would do anything for her child's well-being too. God. She was a mess.

She shoved through the door and into the entry hall, a thousand tasks calling to her that for once, she ignored. She trudged up the stairs, trailing her hand along the polished wood banister, thinking of the times Ashley went sailing down the curved railing. Even shy little Ashley was more of a risk taker.

Practicality kept this place afloat, darn it, not an easy task.

The wallpaper might be peeling, the air conditioner sputtering, but she loved all the space after the cramped apartments and overcrowded shelters of her childhood. Her airy bedroom was a haven.

A haven currently occupied.

She found Starr sprawled back on the chaise longue by the open window with a bag of Jelly Bellies beans in hand. Her sister pitched an unopened bag across the room. "Have fun this morning?"

"Hmm," Claire muttered noncommittally. She clutched the bag and rested against the edge of the mattress, toeing off her shoes one at a time and lining them up side by side. "What are you doing here? I thought you were going home."

"Waiting for the scoop. I came in the back entrance." Starr stretched her jean-clad leg to nudge Claire's shoes off-center.

"Brat."

"Drama queen."

Claire straightened the sandals again. "Inspector says everything is sound. Bad luck over. Not even a black cat through the window."

"Shh! Zip it!" Grinning, Starr pinched her thumb and pointer together and zipped sideways. "Not one more word or next time I'm in the restaurant I'll mix up your recipe box."

"Do it and I'll paint the entire carriage house beige."

Claire tore open her bag of candy. The drifting aroma of sugar made her mouth water. Good heavens, she couldn't remember when she'd been this hungry. Was that her stomach rumbling or more thunder? "How did we spend so long in the same house and turn out so different?"

Starr shrugged, toying with the ends of her braided ribbon belt holding her craft apron in place. "Different paths to deal with the same problems, I guess. You organize and I fantasize."

Claire studied her twenty-four-year-old baby sister who suddenly wasn't such a baby anymore. "When did you become so wise?"

"Must have happened while you were busy alphabetizing your pantry."

Claire swept Starr's legs to the side and sat beside her. "You really are a brat, funny, but a brat."

"A brat who supplied your Jelly Bellies."

"True. I guess I really am a drama queen."

Starr picked up a stray lock of Claire's shoulder-length hair and separated it into three strands for braiding as the skies opened up with rain outside. Claire didn't bother telling her to stop. Chastising Starr was kind of like hitting your head against a wall. Besides, the sisterly ritual brought an odd comfort.

Tears pricked her eyes. More than ever, she wanted to spill everything as fast as the rain drops tinking on the roof.

Her sister twined strand over strand into a perfect plait. "Are you feeling more rested?"

"Yeah. I was just a smidge frazzled from working so hard." She poured a pile of Jelly Bellies on the cushion and sorted by flavor.

"You? Frazzled? No way! That would make you human like the rest of us."

Popping a cappuccino jelly bean in her mouth—as close as she allowed herself to caffeine these days—Claire stared through the open French doors, out over the balcony to where Vic's boat bobbed in the stormy harbor.

"Do you want to tell me what's going on with the two of you?" Starr plaited one strand over the other in a teeny strand. "Or should I say three of you?"

Claire's hand slid to her stomach before she could stop herself. "How did you figure it out? Does anyone else know?"

"I think your secret is safe for now at least. I'm just closer to you than most. Besides, I know the signs since I went through a lot of foster homes before landing here and saw lots of pregnant teenagers."

"I guess the swizzle stick comments weren't so innocent after all. You were digging for info."

"Hoping you would talk to me."

She'd never considered how her silence might hurt her sister. "I'm sorry. I needed to tell Vic first. And I want to be sure he and I are together for the right reasons, not just for the baby. Is that so wrong of me?"

"Baggage sucks." She worked the strands together, the perfection of the tiny braid a funny dichotomy from her disorderly sister.

"What do you mean?"

"It's exhausting always waiting for the next shoe to drop." Starr's hands slowed on the braid, her eyes going distant as she stared out the window, staring at what? The marina and snoopy Ronnie Calhoun? Or the houses next door with those judgmental neighbors and the cranky Mrs. Hamilton-Reis racing inside with her hedge trimmers? "Always knowing happy times are fleeting. Years spent with Aunt Libby couldn't erase all those years of bad luck and the certainty that even if people loved you they would let you down."

"Do you think this is all simply baggage, and I should trust Vic?"

Starr snorted, her attention firmly back in the room and finishing her impromptu hairstyling gig. "Honey, I don't even trust myself. No way am I the one to give you advice." Starr snagged a small rubber band from her bottomless apron pocket that somehow always carried something for every occasion. "Just letting you know you're not nuts for wondering."

"Thank you." For the help. For the braid. For somehow knowing to be there for her. Claire leaned to wrap her arms around her sister. "I love you, brat."

"Love you back." Starr squeezed her for a

quick second, before resting her hand on her sister's stomach. "And love you, too, little one." She smiled at Claire, backing away. "Be happy."

The door clicked closed behind her, echoing in the now empty room.

Happiness.

Why did she have such a tough time believing it would stick around? And then while she waited to trust, she lost it. She'd let her fears rob her of an afternoon with Vic she wanted very much.

Pivoting back to her Jelly Bellies, she snagged her bag off the sofa and raked her perfect piles back inside, determined to gobble fistfuls if she wanted. She would mix up all the flavors while she watched and waited for Vic to return from Mrs. Bethea's.

Then she would spend the rest of the day making love with him, savoring up all the flavors of happiness they could find with each other today. Because Starr was right about her.

She didn't have it inside her to trust in forever.

* * *

Setting the parking brake on his truck, Vic shut off the engine, keeping his eyes well away from his fishing boat in the garage's other spot. He really didn't need those acrobatic memories tumbling through his head this evening.

To resist temptation, he'd even hung around Mrs. Bethea's for supper, a good thing since she'd been worked up worrying about Trooper. The wait, though, had made his shoulder stiffen from where the horse had kicked him, something he never would have let happen if he hadn't been distracted by thoughts of Claire.

Vic snagged his vet bag and left the garage, rolling the door down to shut out the vision he didn't need right now. The sun was sinking into the horizon on a day he'd hoped to end differently. Rays sparked off leftover puddles from the short-lived spring shower.

He hoped Claire's anger would be as quickly

spent. Waiting until morning to see her could just about kill him, but he'd vowed to give her space and he kept his promises.

He'd known she was prideful, prickly even, but he admired her determination and her nurturing heart. Lumbering down the dock, he just didn't understand how he could take care of her without sending her running in the other direction faster than those gulls zipping along the shoreline. Sonya had been more than happy to leave details like home inspections to him.

Claire was obviously different, and man, he was such a sap he was seeing Claire around every corner until even the woman standing near his boat looked…like…

Her.

Well, damn. Claire was waiting for him in a flowing cotton sundress, wind plastering the fabric to her body, outlining the gentle curves of her pregnancy… And was that a bag of Jelly

Bellies clutched in her fist? She never stopped surprising him.

"Hey, lady, I thought we weren't going to deal with our problems until tomorrow."

"Kinda tough not to think about you since I have your baby inside me."

"That you do."

At least she was willing to acknowledge that much.

The sunset played with the lighter streaks through her caramel-colored hair. "How's Mrs. Bethea's horse?"

Small talk? Okay, he could go with that. "Her horse really had a problem this time."

"I wondered if maybe that was the case since you were gone a long time."

She'd been watching for him all afternoon? Interesting.

Claire nodded toward his boat. "Do you, uh, mind if we talk inside?"

What was she up to? Regardless, the ice pack

for his bruised shoulder would have to wait. "Sure. Come on up."

She fit her hand in his. He stifled a wince as he helped her on deck. He'd been hurt worse in the course of his job—broken ribs coming immediately to mind. He vaulted up beside her, which really hurt like hell but no way did he want to lose out on this time with her by sending her off so he could tend a stupid bruise. He swept open the hatch and gestured her through.

She gripped the rail on her way into his galley/living area. "Nothing serious, I hope, with the horse, I mean."

"An abscess in his hoof. Not life threatening, just painful." In more ways than one for both of them. "At least it wasn't Hoof Wall Disease, which is far more complicated to treat."

Pivoting, she studied him as he carefully made his way down. "Are you okay?"

"I'm fine." Thank goodness he'd cleaned up around here earlier in anticipation of their post-doctor plans, counters on the right clean, table on the other side set with a platter of strawberries and chocolate. Deeper inside, the sofa called with extra pillows.

And he so didn't need to think about his bed a few steps away.

"Really?" She thunked her bag of Jelly Bellies down onto the counter beside two wine glasses he'd planned to fill with milk. "Then you won't mind if I return the massage favor and rub *your* back—"

He must have stepped away without thinking because she crossed her arms under her gorgeous, gorgeous breasts, nodding. "Yeah, right, you're okay. What's going on with your shoulder?"

"Abscesses hurt. The horse got torqued off, and I didn't duck in time. No big deal." He shrugged. Winced. He was so busted. "Trooper clipped me on the shoulder."

"Omigod!" She raced closer, her hands

hovering in midair as if trying to determine a safe spot to land. "Are you sure you're all right? Did you see a doctor?"

"I *am* a doctor, and I'm fine." Just aching to take her clothes off and wondering why she was here when they'd left things so unsettled. "No broken bones, only a helluva bruise."

"*Only* a bruise?" she gasped. Her fingers flew to the hem of his polo shirt and inched upward, hesitating halfway up his chest. "Careful, okay? I'm going to slip this off your arm—" She scrunched fabric and eased one arm through "—and over your head."

With a tender care that stirred him and spooked him all at once, she gently worked the shirt off his injured side. Her soft hands skimmed over his heated skin, stirring more heat lower down. Standing as close as she was, she couldn't possibly miss his erection throbbing against his jean zipper with painful intensity.

Her sexy little gasp as she froze with his shirt

bunched in her hands against her chest told him she hadn't missed a thing.

He stepped closer, heat to heat. "Lady, if you want to get me naked, you only have to ask."

Seven

Oh, she wanted Vic, all right. Naked. On his bed in the next room, tangled up in that blue-and-green striped spread. Or anywhere here in the galley for that matter, as long as it was soon.

First she needed to check his shoulder where the horse had kicked him. Tough to do when the power of his eyes held her as firmly as the heat of his body grazing against hers. His bare chest broad and sprinkled with blond hair, toned pecs and the scent of masculine sweat—

Stop. At this rate she would jump him in a heartbeat. One step at a time, she pried herself away and around until she saw—

Claire gasped. "That bruise looks horrible." Her hand trembling, she raised it to hover over the purple-and-green stain stretching across his shoulder blade. "You're gonna hurt something fierce by tomorrow."

"I hurt like hell tonight," he mumbled.

Her stomach roiled far harder than during her worst bout of morning sickness. She needed to get a hold of her flipping tummy now, but calling on all her old Claire efficiency proved darn near impossible as her logical mind blared with the horrific possibility of that stray kick catching Vic in the head instead.

She rushed to the freezer and pulled out the ice bucket. "Have you taken anything for the pain?"

He worked his muscled arm gingerly in a circle. "A couple of Motrin."

"You should have something stronger."

"I'm allergic."

Yeah, right. Not that the big lug was listening to her. "More like a testosterone-induced allergy, I'll bet."

"You may have a point."

She suspected he was toughing out the pain because of a macho need to watch over her rather than sleep through the healing. She would simply have to take over, something she did well. "Do you have an ice pack?"

"It's somewhere around here. I can always just use a rag."

Yanking open drawer after drawer, she found a Ziploc bag and dumped ice inside before wrapping the whole makeshift ice pack in a dish towel. She rested the bundle against his shoulder. His jaw flexed, but he stayed silent.

Prideful male. While silence echoed inside the boat, waves slapped outside, along with early evening foot traffic on the dock.

He reached over his shoulder and took the

makeshift ice pack, sagging to sit at the small galley table. "Can I take your presence here as a sign that I'm forgiven for hiring the inspector behind your back?"

"Let's just say that while I do not agree with your decision, I can see how perhaps you may have thought I wouldn't be open to discussing the matter."

"Okay. Where do we go from here?"

Hopefully to his bed to enjoy what time together they could before they *had* to make the tough decisions.

"Before the baby is born, we need to have things decided." She slid her hand behind him and took over holding the pack. "I don't want our child living in an uncertain world of us in an on-again, off-again relationship. So the way I see it, we have a window of time here to explore whatever feelings we may have for each other and see where they lead."

His eyes lit a second before he tugged her

into his lap. "You're telling me I have the next few months to win you over."

"Argh. No." She resisted the urge to punch his arm since he was injured. Besides, his lap did seem like a nice place to rest at the moment. "This isn't about putting on some big show. We need to get to know each other better."

"We've been friends for months already." His arms banded loosely around her.

"But if you really knew me, you would realize how very much I resented your taking control of my life by calling that inspector." Why not stay put on his lap against his yummy bare chest, a comfy place to have this discussion? If she could keep her brain engaged to important facts. "And I would have known your ex-wife's name. We need to build trust."

"Fair enough." He skimmed a hand up and down her arm. "Does this courtship mean we can't have sex?"

Facts, schmacts. She'd already decided to

enjoy every moment she could with him. Why segment her life? Like mixing up her Jelly Bellies, she could enjoy sex with Vic as they were getting to know each other.

Her hand clenching around the frigid ice pack, she arched back and pitched it in the sink. "We can most definitely have sex."

The clunk of the ice pack in the sink echoed through the small galley and Vic's head.

Finally, he had Claire in his arms—or on his lap—in a boat again. And the boat was bigger this time, with more space to explore her luscious body and hopefully not mess things up.

As much as he wanted to go straight for her mouth, he reined himself in for a slower approach, dipping his face in the crook of her neck. Her sigh, followed by a whimper-moan rewarded him. Her arms looped around his waist, her fingers tucking into the waistband of his jeans.

He scrunched fabric in his hands, tugging

until her loose sundress swept up and over her head. Her lacy underwear echoed the amazing image of her in her bathing suit the day before, except champagne lace gave peekaboo hints of taboo flesh.

Gracing her neck with another nip that rose goose bumps on her skin, he skimmed lower to close his mouth over her nipple, laving a damp spot on the creamy fabric. His hand worked equal attention on her other breast, using the combination of touch and subtle abrasion of the lace.

Panting, she cupped his face and urged him nearer, more pressure and yeah, he liked a woman who knew what she wanted. She flicked her flip-flops off to thud on the water-resistant carpet. If her tormenting squirming in his lap was anything to judge by, they both very much wanted the same thing.

Claire guided his face up to her mouth, whispering her need between frantic kisses. He reached behind her to release her bra in a smooth sweep that left them naked chest to chest.

Closer, closer again she wriggled, her face puckering with a frustrated smile. "I'm not as limber as I was a few months ago."

He gripped her hips. "I actually happen to know quite a lot about how to work around a growing stomach."

Her smile faded. She looked down and away, the thin navy-blue carpet suddenly capturing her total attention.

Way to go, moron, mentioning the ex-wife during a naked moment with another woman. "That was really idiotic of me."

"Don't be silly." She scavenged half her smile back, almost chasing away the shadows in her dark eyes. "We come to each other with pasts. You were married before. I was engaged once. Neither of us can wish that away."

"And you would wish away my marriage to Sonya?" Hey, wait. Claire had been engaged?

"Sonya? That was her name?"

"I'm sorry for never mentioning it before." He hated talking about that time.

The shadows deepened. "The omission did make me wonder if you're really over her."

How could he have totally missed her assuming something so far off base? Of course, Sonya had always said his communication skills sucked when it came to humans. She'd undoubtedly been right. He knew better than to put all the blame on her for the marriage failing—a hell he didn't want to repeat.

He shook off the past before it spooked Claire from his lap. He would learn from his mistakes, damn it. "I can assure you I am completely over Sonya." Communication ran both ways, lady. "And this fiancé *you've* never mentioned before. Does that mean you're not really over Mr. No Name?"

Pink tinged her face and shoulders. Embarrassment? Or regret. "I never mentioned Ross because he is such a jackass. I am totally over him and rarely think of him."

"A jackass?" Relief kicked him harder than the horse. She wasn't regretting at all. She was gloriously angry. As quickly as the relief hit, he considered another possibility. "How so? Did he hurt you?"

"Not physically, so you can back down." She smoothed her hands over his chest in a feather-light touch that seared through to his gut, and uh, why were they talking? "Ross just up and decided he didn't want to get married. No reason other than, 'Whoops. Sorry. I don't really love you after all.'"

He knew that pain well, finding out the person you'd expected to stand by you no matter what didn't have it in them for the long haul. It truly was better not needing anyone. "I'm sorry you were hurt."

"And I am sorry you were hurt and betrayed

in a way that goes so much deeper than stupid old Ross."

Her unselfish acknowledgement stirred something in him. He was so used to taking care of others, it felt strange having someone put him first. Unsettling, too, because he was far more comfortable being in control.

This conversation was getting too deep, especially when they were half-naked. In fact, he'd "communicated" more with Claire in these past few days than he had in his whole life.

He took her mouth again and thank goodness she got the message, her palm flattening to the fly of his jeans. He growled his encouragement against her lips. Her hands made fast work of his belt and zipper, opening his pants then—oh, yeah—she freed him from his boxers.

With her nipples tight against his chest and him throbbing against the juncture of her satiny thighs, surely they were both due the much-needed relief of some nonverbal communication.

* * *

Vic's hands hot against her bare skin, Claire breathed a sigh of relief as he slanted his mouth over hers.

As much as she'd wanted reassurance he was over his ex-wife, the deeper waters were threatening to suck her into something scary. So many people had simply told her she was well rid of Ross, and how lucky that she'd found out before they married. While she knew they were right, that didn't stop the pain of the betrayal. Vic's quiet acknowledgment touched her in a way no one else ever had.

And speaking of touching… "Hmm… Do that again."

She encouraged his hand to keep right on moving lower until he hooked a finger in her panties. She figured he could take it from there… Or rather take it *off*.

Inching backward, she slid from his knees to stand so he could sweep her underwear down to her ankles. She kicked the lacy scrap free, enjoying the view of him lounging back watching her watch him. Her toes curled against the bristly carpet. Her gaze fell to his lap and given that throb, he had no problems with what he saw.

She extended a hand for him. "Since you're an expert on inventive positions, which would you like to start with?"

"Start?" He hooked his fingers with hers, still sitting. "As in we'll get to try out more than one?"

"If you're up to it."

"Lady, after waiting for you for months, I suspect I'll be up for plenty."

Her legs wobbled. "You haven't been with anyone else since that night?"

"You live next door." He tugged her back between his knees, jeans open but not off. "You should know."

"I thought." She squeezed his hand. "I hoped. But I didn't want to assume."

"You are welcome to assume that since I first saw you, I haven't wanted any other woman." He cupped her waist and lifted her up to straddle his lap again. "Right here. Right now."

Squealing, she braced her hands against the boat wall behind him, the fabric of his pants a sexy, forbidden abrasion against her bare thighs. "What about your shoulder?"

"The last thing I'm thinking about is my shoulder." He brought her hand to his straining arousal.

"I have to agree." She angled up, her knees sinking into the upholstered cushion, then eased down to take him inside her. No boundaries. Bodies and emotions bare and raw as the need hammering through her veins.

He moved in, out, in again with a gentle strength. His care touching her heart as intensely as his hands stroked her breasts, as hotly as his breath caressed her ears with a rambling litany of how much he wanted her. How much she turned him inside out needing to be inside her. Deeper. Repeatedly.

How could she be so sure of him, of them, here and doubt the minute they were apart? If only she didn't have to step off the boat or out of her house and they could while away days on end making love.

His hands roved up to cup her breasts, thumbs and forefingers rolling, tugging until she ached to be closer. She arched forward into his palms, worked her hips against him, wanting more of everything until *yesss*... Vic's ragged breaths thrilled her. Her own huffing gasps pressing her more firmly into his touch.

Until... Her perfectly ordered world flew apart in the shattering power of her release with near-painful tingling along her hypersensitive skin. Her hands clutched his thickly muscled arms, fingers digging deep for anchor.

Sagging against his chest while aftershocks

rippled through her, she gasped for air. "So was this one of the inventive positions?"

"Yes, ma'am." He soothed circles over her back. "It's a good start on my list."

List? She liked the sound of that, but after she closed her eyes for a little while longer.

Next thing she knew she was floating. Literally. Scooped up in Vic's arms, she languished in the weightless feeling, a good thing since her mellow muscles wouldn't have carried her. "You're really starting to make a habit of this macho carrying-me-around stuff."

"It's a habit I wouldn't mind continuing for years to come."

She couldn't miss the subtle pressure but she refused to let it ruin this moment. In fact, she couldn't deny the warmth seeping through her at the thought of being in Vic's arms again. She was all about savoring the moment tonight.

He lowered her onto his bed before sliding in beside her. Staring at the stars through the narrow rectangular window, she could see how the boat would be great for getaways from the world and obligations, but she wondered how he'd managed to stay here for months on end without becoming claustrophobic. As luxurious as his boat might be, she knew she could never live in a place like this. After a few days she would need the airy spaciousness of her home the same way he seemed to crave this rootless life.

Would he feel the same restlessness in her home that she felt now?

She didn't doubt his innate honor for even a second. He wouldn't turn his back on her or their baby, and she had to admire that quality after the way her father, Ross and truly every man she'd ever known had let her down. However, would Vic be happy? The more she knew him, the more important that became. A truly scary thought.

Whoops.

There went the moment.

* * *

The moment the arctic—glacial, freaking frigid—ice pack hit his shoulder, Vic bolted upright in his bed. Awake now. Totally awake from a nightmare of losing Emma *and* the new baby while swimming here in Charleston, which made no sense because Emma had never left North Dakota. "Jeez, Claire, could you have made that any colder?"

He swung his legs over the edge of the mattress, sheet tangled around his waist. Fishing a hand through the covers in the dark, he gathered up the ice pack from where it had fallen on the bed.

Claire plopped cross-legged beside him, wearing one of his overlong Cornell University T-shirts, the shirt ghostly white with only moonlight streaking through the portal. "That's why they call it ice."

"Sorry." He dropped a kiss on her forehead, mentally kicking himself for letting his edginess show. "Didn't mean to bite your head off."

An edginess she obviously shared. The sex had been intense, to say the least, even more than before, which shouldn't have been possible. He'd been so focused on the stakes for their baby, he hadn't given much thought to the two of them. And didn't that just validate every concern Claire had voiced?

The remains of their strawberry and Jelly Belly meal on the tray by the bed reminded him of smiles and fun with sex, something he suspected serious Claire hadn't indulged in often.

He dipped his head to nibble on her shoulder. "Although maybe you wouldn't mind if I bit a little."

Claire's smile flickered, then faltered. Her gaze trotted away, down to her hands where she picked at a loose thread on the spread. "I understand that you wanted to be near your sister and her family, but why a boat and not a new house?"

His boat? She wanted to talk about where he

lived? He searched for the trick in her question and couldn't track the path of her thinking yet, especially in the middle of the night.

"What more do I need?" Ah, hell. He'd walked right into the pit even while looking for it. "I meant, uh, I didn't need anything more before."

She didn't move away. A good sign. Maybe he hadn't screwed up too badly.

"If I'd said yes to your proposal, where would we have lived?"

She might be speaking in the hypothetical, but he couldn't miss the underlying implica-tion. His answer was important and obvious. "I assumed we would live in your place. I'm not much for being a kept man, so we would have to work something out financially with me paying bills."

"It would get complicated."

"We're smart people."

Her hands rested over her stomach in a pro-tective—and possessive?—gesture. "Everyone would say I married you for your money and because you knocked me up."

This conversation was derailing. Fast. Time to reroute. He nuzzled her neck, tasting residual strawberry juice on her skin. "Or maybe they would say I married you for your hot body."

Her head fell back to give him freer access to her throat. "And my iced tea."

"There is that."

She shifted in his arms, ducking to meet his eyes. "Part of my business is a bar."

"I noticed."

"Is that a problem for you?"

No wonder she had concerns. All he could do on this one was be honest. "It hasn't been yet." He searched for the right way to sum up something he was still taking a day at a time. "I guess you could say I'm like that character on an old sitcom, the guy who faced down his alcoholism by being a bartender."

"Like how you face down Emma's

drowning by living on the water every day of your life."

Her words blindsided him, coming hard and fast on the heels of his nightmare.

"Vic, wait. I'm sorry." She squeezed his knee, her touch sending a jolt through his suddenly hypersensitive nerves. "I shouldn't have said that. I didn't even know I was thinking it until the words fell out."

"No harm, no foul," he clipped out, already off the bed and reaching for a pair of running shorts. "Do you want something to eat? I'm still hungry."

Tugging on the shorts, he made tracks toward the galley, not a far walk at all and somehow he found himself up on deck rather than at the fridge scrounging for a couple of apples and a jar of peanut butter. Could there be truth in her words? He'd certainly told himself the water made him feel closer to Emma because she enjoyed fishing and boating. Could he have chosen this lifestyle as some sort of twisted penance? He wasn't sure he liked what that said about his frame of mind, especially when he was looking at fatherhood again soon.

Was he looking at marriage again as well?

His gaze skipped like a stone over the water until he looked at Beachcombers and tried to picture himself living there. Two stories with attic eaves, a lot of square footage calling to make memories inside, trees hollering for a tire swing or hammock. The more memories a guy made, the more remained to haunt him when it all blew up. Ghostly shadows that stretched through the night.

Shadows. His brain hitched on the word, warning him to look closer at Claire's home. He scanned, searched, found…

A dark-clad person lurked on the bar porch, peering inside her window.

Eight

Resisting the urge to kick herself for being so insensitive and mentioning Vic's daughter, Claire scrambled off the bed. She still thought her perception of why he'd moved to the boat was correct, but voicing it wouldn't accomplish anything.

The man had been dealt a horribly painful blow by fate. Who was she to judge him for coping the best he could?

What a tricky balance to figure out how to get

to know him well enough to trust, while respecting his boundaries. Come to think of it, how many close friendships had she cultivated to learn the skill? Only Tina, Aunt Libby, her two sisters… And hey, wait, why hadn't she listed Ross?

A telling omission.

She'd been terrified of giving her heart to a man all her life. Her hand fell to rest on her stomach.

Everything was different now. She couldn't keep her distance any longer. Her child needed a brave mama, not one who cowered below deck because her relationship with a man got complicated.

Claire shimmied into her sundress and made her way to the steps.

The hatch sealed with the bulk of Vic's body outside. "Claire, call the cops, then wait here."

"Cops?" Huh?

"Someone's snooping around your house."

A prowler? Panic mingled with anger to squeeze her ribs, constricting breathing.

"Omigod, I'll get the phone for you." She spun back, cellphone in hand, to find him gone. "Vic? Vic!"

She scrambled up to the deck. Vic was already halfway down the dock, with nothing but his hands and a battered shoulder to take on whatever waited at her place.

Her fingers shaking, she dialed 911 and called in the emergency as she looked around the deck for something, anything to help Vic. She had to be careful for their baby, but she couldn't simply sit here and wait. She relayed the details to the emergency operator, never taking her eyes off Vic.

Until he disappeared around the back of her home.

Panic and anger quickly morphed to outright fear. What he was facing even now? He was so confident in everything he did, would he realize that he wasn't invulnerable to a bullet or knife?

What about her sister? Claire disconnected with the operator and punched in Starr's number. Pick up. Pick up. Pick up…

"Hello?" Starr answered, breathy. Freshly woken?

"There's someone prowling around outside. Vic is on his own checking it out—"

"Stay calm. I'm sending David out now."

David? Her sister was with David Hamilton-Reis again and hadn't even mentioned it? Or was it another David? Something to think on—later. "Thank you. Stay safe."

Thumbing off the phone, Claire stepped from the boat and started down the dock. If nothing else she could rouse help from the other boaters and the marina owner.

Just as she opened her mouth to shout, Vic rounded the corner of her house. Alone. She gasped gulps of relief. Running, she met him at the base of the dock, her hands skimming over him, finding nothing wrong, and still her heart pumped. "Are you…? Is everything…? What happened?"

"Baby, slow down." He clasped her shoulders. "Take a deep breath. Nothing happened. Whoever it was ran off before he could do anything more than cut out a windowpane."

"I don't care about the house. You could have been hurt." Gingerly, she touched his shoulder. "You've already been injured once today."

Starr's porch lights blared on in the pitch dark, the front door of her carriage house swinging open, with a man behind her. Oops. Except her sister wore frayed jean shorts and one of her hand-painted Beachcombers T-shirts, not bedclothes and she certainly didn't look as if she'd just rolled out of bed. The man stepped into the porch light.

As she'd suspected, Starr's old boyfriend, David Hamilton-Reis. Or rather David Reis, since he'd dropped the whole double-name thing, disclaiming his mother's lifestyle as easily as he sought to rid himself of his family's house.

If he and Starr weren't sleeping together again, what had they been talking about at four in the morning? It seemed a strange time to discuss his impending house sale.

Certainly he would stand to benefit from seeing her house sold off to a land developer, thus upping the price of his land. And severing Starr's ties to the house, leaving her free to follow him, one of the things that had broken them up in the past...

She hated doubting everyone.

Sirens sounded—yet again, heading to her place for the second time in less than a week, drawing the neighbors from their homes for another round of checking out a ruckus at Beachcombers.

But right now, concerns about their business reputation were nothing up against her nauseat-

ing fear that something could happen to Vic.
Her emotions were growing more tangled by the
moment and she still had no idea how he felt.

Sunrise peeking from the shoreline, Vic stood
at the base of the marina dock. He watched the
last of the neighbors return to their homes and
the marina owner climb back into his boat. Vic
palmed Claire's waist. For comfort, of course.

And so she wouldn't hightail it off the beach
and back into her house before they could get a
few issues straight.

The cops had found a couple of stray footprints around the shrubbery and a fingerprint on
the pane, all of which could have been made by
patrons so it didn't tell them squat. Starr and the
guy staying with her—her old neighbor?—
hadn't seen a thing since apparently they'd
been otherwise occupied. The Reis fellow was
polite enough, worked a civilian job at Charleston Air Force Base. But the guy was holding

something back and that made Vic hesitant to trust him totally.

Of course, was there anybody he would totally trust to watch over Claire?

He slid his arm around her waist and tucked her to his side. "Wanna watch the sunrise?" He nodded toward the Beachcombers pier that stretched alongside the marina dock.

"Sure, no need to go back to sleep now, right?" Side by side, the walked along the shoreline. Her flip-flops dangled from her hand as they picked their way around sea oats toward the pier.

Gulls dive-bombed for breakfast, swooping upward again. Marsh grass rustled in the silence between them as Claire paused to scoop through the grains of sand for a spiral-shaped shell. Silence with her felt better than conversation with anyone else. He hated to disrupt that, but he couldn't avoid what needed to be done.

"I've been thinking." He knelt beside her, sifting sand through his fingers, so different from North Dakota soil, but he was learning to like it equally as well. Dirt was dirt. People were what counted. "I'm going to take a week off from work. Since I'm worried about your place and you won't let me pay anyone to help you, I'll hang out with you."

"Whoa." Her head jerked up. "Hold on. You can't just move in."

Vic palmed the slight swell of her stomach where their child rested. Would he have the right to touch her through all stages of this pregnancy? "Are you saying you don't want to spend the week with me?"

She covered his hand with hers. "I'm not sure how logically I'll be able think if we're together *all* the time."

He didn't want her thinking logically anymore because if she did, he'd be out on his butt in a heartbeat. Heaven knew, he felt anything but *logical* around her. "And we were making progress apart?"

"You're right. I'm being prickly when we have important issues to discuss and work out for the baby. How about we take this a day at a time?"

"Can do." Rising, Vic extended his hand, clasping hers and starting down the planked pier.

Their footsteps echoed from below where waves lapped at the pilings with the gushing tide. At the end, she stopped. Digging into her pocket, she scooped out the shells and lined them up alongside others on the rail.

Vic stood behind her while she finished her Claire-on-a-budget decorating. The salty wind picked up her loose hair, teasing it back against him. A lone boat trawled in the distance, and yeah, the scenery was a complete opposite of the North Dakota plains. But the broad expanse of endless ocean proved no less freaking amazing.

He could enjoy a lot of sunrises with this woman. "I thought we'd planned on a week for you to think about my proposal. The only thing that's changing is where I sleep." A mighty big something. "That will give the police a chance to look into things."

"Where will you be sleeping?" She inched the shells into perfect alignment.

"Hopefully with you."

Her hand stilled. "Uh—"

"But that's not a deal breaker if you would prefer I hang out in one of your guest rooms."

"Pack a bag." She dusted the sand from her hands. "The bedroom thing, well, I know it seems silly since we've already slept together, but sharing a bed long-term would be the same as living together. That's just a step I'm not ready to take yet. Okay?"

She stared into his eyes. Was she waiting for him to say something? If so, what? Did she want him to be a knuckle-dragger and demand she change her mind? But he saw something else in her eyes, something that looked a little like a question. An expectation of…

Practical Claire couldn't actually want him to roll out pretty words. Or could she?

From the start, they'd been about friendship and, yeah, attraction. But they had never been about romance.

Just that fast the clue bird smacked him upside the head. They'd had the friendship and sex parts pretty well licked. Outings on his boat were nice, but hadn't made significant inroads toward winning her over.

Maybe practical Claire could be wooed by a bit of dazzle after all.

Wiped out from a killer workday and virtually no sleep the night before, Claire blinked past the sparks in her eyes from the refrigerator light cutting across her dark kitchen. The last of the customers were gone from the restaurant—thank goodness they didn't keep the bar open on Tuesdays through Thursdays—and she needed a cold glass of milk before bed to meet her calcium quota.

She listened to Vic's even treads throughout the house as he checked the newly installed, upgraded locks. He may have taken time off from work, but he certainly hadn't relaxed for a second of it.

He'd spent the day conferring with David about ways to improve security on the restaurant and carriage house. Then out came the hammers and screwdrivers and holy cow, muscles started flexing.

Except while the muscles were appealing, he'd also been at his most charming all day. He'd pruned her herb garden, his North Dakota farm days resurfacing in a majorly helpful way when he'd added an aloe plant for her frequent kitchen burns. He'd even mentioned taking her out to a shell island, loaded with decorative possibilities. The romanticism mixed images of making love on the beach all day long.

She tipped her face into the frosty blast of the fridge. Forget milk. Where was the ice cream? She yanked open the freezer and rooted around.

"Look behind that ice sculpture of a swan there."

Vic's voice rumbled through the darkened kitchen and over her senses. How could he turn her on with just his voice?

"Thank you." She inched aside the romantic birds and found…

Ohh. Thin-mint ice cream. Her favorite and an indulgence she rarely fed. She usually opted for the value tubs of Neapolitan. So where had this come from?

From the man who'd told her to look behind the ice sculpture.

Pride be damned, she was going to enjoy every bite. Claire clasped the cold container to her chest and spun around. "You totally rock, Vic Jansen."

"Doing my best, ma'am."

She hip-bumped the refrigerator closed before her swans liquefied and she lost her sculpture for the extravagant rehearsal dinner on Friday. Her big event. And what if her power went out and this cost-a-fortune ice sculpture melted? She so needed to save for a backup generator for her refrigerator.

"Claire. Let it go."

"Huh?" She jerked her attention back to him at the counter.

"Work is done." He plucked a spoon from a bin on the counter and passed it to her. "Let it go and revel in a successful business day."

And a successful first day of sorta, not really, living together.

She couldn't get enough of looking at him either, especially after the prowler scare. So many emotions jumbled inside her. How would he adapt to her house if she invited him in long-term? And how should she deal with all these growing feelings?

He should be important to her. He was the father of her baby, after all.

Why hadn't he been more disappointed over not sharing a bed? And why was she so disappointed over his easy acceptance? She couldn't escape the sense that she was being maneuvered. Yet with her heart still pounding from fear for him, she figured she could simply enjoy his company for now and figure out the rest later.

She had ice cream to eat and she refused to worry about her waistline, which was unmistakably expanding daily now.

Claire sagged into the chair Vic had pulled out for her. "Thank you for changing the locks. I really do feel safer with you here."

"I'm glad." He straddled a chair across from her.

She spooned a taste straight from the carton. Minty chocolate flooded her senses. Man, food tasted so much better when she was pregnant.

"Who could want to hurt me? I really can't think of anyone. And actually, other than the gas leak, none of the accidents were potentially lethal."

"Didn't you say the gas leak happened on one of the worst possible days of the week?"

"As if deliberately planned." She shuddered, her mind sifting through scenarios like ingredients for one of her recipes as she sought to put it all together.

"I'm going to ask a question and please don't take this wrong or get your knickers in a twist."

Her spoon paused mid-bite. "You're making me nervous."

"How financially devastating was it to be closed for a day? Sunday, in particular?"

"It's not good." She dug out a heaping bite. "But we can survive it—as long as nothing happens like that again."

"Who stands to profit if you go out of business?" His hands folded over the back of the chair, he rested his chin on his wrists.

"There have always been people who want this piece of land, and of course the larger corporations who want the whole street to build condos. Except they will only buy if they can have my lot as well."

"And they'll just plow the historic homes?"

"The ones they can. The ones protected by the historical registry will be used as clubhouses and such."

"So basically, any of the Hamilton-Reis kids, the marina owner or the entire neighborhood would benefit from closing you down."

"Seems so." She closed the ice cream, even thin-mint chocolate not enough to camouflage the acrid taste of a suspected someone nearby wanting to hurt her.

"What about your sisters?"

"What do you mean?"

"Selling the place could bring you all three a nice chunk of change."

Anger—and flat-out hurt—stole through

her. "How dare you accuse them! They are
my sisters."

"Just asking if maybe free-spirited Starr feels
constrained by the strictures of running her own
business. And what about Ashley? She could
finance her whole college education."

Anger sparked hotter along already vulnerable nerves. Echoes of all those old neighborhood sly looks and whispers rolled
through her head.

But worst of all, even while she knew her
sisters wouldn't do anything to harm her, what
if she'd been hurting them by pushing *her*
dream for the house onto them? Her guilt
swelled like yeasty dough.

"They wouldn't do anything to sabotage our
business."

"Hey, you know them better than I do."
Standing, he tucked his chair under the table and
crossed to her. "If you say they couldn't be guilty
of anything, then that's good enough for me."

"Thank you." Her anger deflated, if not her guilt.

He was only trying to help, and she was edgy over climbing the stairs and going to separate rooms.

She clicked lights off on their way to the entry hall, blanketing the house in darkness other than the moonlight streaking through the over-large window at the top of the staircase. The intimacy to the moment, the stars and solitude streamed over her as well.

That, and the memory of how they'd made love on the staircase nearly four months ago, so hot for each other.

They really had made some amazing memories—as well as a child—that weekend. What might have happened if she hadn't run scared from the intensity of her feelings then? What kind of trust might they have built when they never had to wonder if a pregnancy brought them together?

She didn't know. But she *did* know that he was trying and it was time for her to try, too. Really try.

This seemed like a good time to give him the gift she'd put together halfway through a restless afternoon waiting for him. "Hang on a second."

Claire tucked into her room, racing over to the mahogany secretary desk.

"Here." She pulled a tissue-wrapped package from behind her stationery. "I know you don't have a lot of room on your boat, but I thought you might like to have this."

He loomed in the door. "For me?"

"It's nothing fancy." She passed him the wrapped three-by-two frame with the ultrasound picture inside. "Just something I put together while you were at Mrs. Bethea's."

He peeled away the tissue and froze.

Watching him cradle it in his hands… *Gulp.* Her heart melted faster than leftover ice cream.

"The frame is one of Starr's custom-crafted items from the gift shop, which I thought made the whole thing all the more special, given that she's family. I've been thinking about the name and wondered if you wanted to use your sister's name for a girl. Elizabeth Paige Jansen."

"I like it. The name and the frame. Thanks."

He dipped his head, pressed a lingering, closed-mouth kiss to her lips and—

Left? She swayed.

The guest room door clicked closed behind him. He was really going to sleep in the other room. Even after all the times they'd made love, still she wanted more, her breasts heavy and aching for his touch.

So just call out to him.

Yet a part of her also wanted more time with the ice cream and the look in his eyes that said he was only seeing her. Only her.

What an unsettling notion to consider that

maybe men hadn't always let her down. Perhaps she'd been the one bailing out first before risking another hurt. She refused to be a person who blamed others for her problems. But maybe, just maybe, she'd been more scarred than she thought by her father's rejection. A man she'd never even met, and somehow she'd taken that out on every other significant male to cross her path.

Wow. Self-realization stunk.

She wanted to bolt through the door and tell Vic what she'd figured out. Except they would land in bed together at a time when they needed more than ever to explore the emotions. She needed to return to her original plan. Spend the next few days together, working together, thinking.

His footsteps echoed in the next room, just a simple slab of plaster away. She flattened her hand to the wall, flocked paper bristly against her hand almost like a five o'clock shadow.

Sheesh, she was in sad shape if even wallpaper reminded her of Vic.

It was going to be a long week until her Friday deadline.

Nine

T.G.I.F.

Vic hoped.

The bedside clock flickered to 12:01, glowing beside the shell-framed ultrasound photo. Midnight. Officially Friday.

He lounged back on the guest-room bed, a simple room, with sparse furniture and a white cotton spread. Claire had obviously taken all the best pieces downstairs. Yet she had more in this room than he had on his whole sailboat.

Although his air conditioner on the boat certainly worked better than the ancient window unit sputtering away.

Where would he park his butt after tonight? Claire's room or back in his seafaring home? There hadn't been any further security incidents, so he doubted she would go for the protection excuse much longer.

After the rehearsal dinner tonight, Claire's insanely hectic week would be over and she would make her decision one way or another. He liked to think that even if she said no now, he could persuade her in the coming months. However, Claire was decisive. Once she made up her mind, she forged ahead, like with this business.

Claire could tackle whatever she wanted with success. He respected that trait in her. He just wasn't sure she planned to pour that energy and drive into the two of them.

Sleeping in the next room had been torturous.

Waking hours, however, had been surprisingly easy. Somehow *right*.

She did need help here. He'd oiled squeaky hinges, nailed in loose shingles.

Installed new locks.

There was an offer pending on the Hamilton-Reis place, so perhaps the issues of selling to the condo group would ease, and thereby, the need to run her out of business. Still, he hated the thought that they might never know who'd sabotaged her house.

He refused to accept that. If someone had attempted to tamper with her business, that person had to pay.

A thud sounded through the wall, followed by a soft curse.

Vic shot from the bed to his feet. Images of her unconscious on the floor flashed through his mind—like earlier that week, the day he'd learned about the baby. Or what if someone was breaking in? Either way, she needed him.

Ten strides later he burst through her bedroom door.

Claire knelt on that flowery chaise of hers in front of the window air conditioner wall unit, a hammer in hand. "Vic?"

He sprinted across the room, sweeping aside the curtains to check outside. "Did you hear someone?"

Did she intend to bash that person's brains in, for goodness sake? Spunky, but a gruesome alternative she wouldn't need to resort to as long as he was around. He tucked her behind him as he scanned the yard.

"Vic!"

"What?" He glanced over his shoulder.

"My air conditioner's broken. I was giving it a good thunk." Her face scrunched in a disgruntled frown as she set the hammer on her end table by a bowl of glossy rocks and dried flower petals. "It always worked in the past. I've nursed all these old window units along as best I could. I won't be able to get away with fans and open windows much longer."

He chewed back the obvious answer kicking around in his gut.

"What?" She stepped back, hands on her hips and, *gulp, hello, libido,* check out her pink knees peeking from under the hem of her long pink Beachcombers T-shirt. "You're not even going to offer to pay for repairs or a whole new central system?"

"You've made yourself clear on that subject." He rested his hand on the dormant AC, instead of reaching for her. "Do you mind if I take a look at it? I assume sweat equity is okay since you didn't object to me crawling around under your house or installing locks."

She chewed her bottom lip, perspiration trickling a tempting path down her throat, past the neck of her T-shirt. He remembered well how overheated Sonya got during her pregnancy. Claire just needed a pride-saving nudge.

"If you're cooler, my baby is cooler."

She released her lip, with a tantalizingly slow return to fullness, and what a time to remember that pregnancy hormones could supercharge her libido as well.

Except he couldn't ever remember anything being as amazing with Sonya as even one time with Claire. The thought alone felt vaguely disloyal. He'd been married to the woman. He should have felt more for her, more over the loss of their relationship. Instead at the end, he'd just felt…hollow.

Enough. He needed to stop comparing the two women. It wasn't fair to either of them. "So? Ready to pass me the hammer?"

She placed the tool on top of the AC. "I appreciate that you're an honorable man who wants to be there for his child. Believe me, after the way I grew up, that is something I definitely don't take for granted. Still I can't help but wonder. Would you be here if I wasn't pregnant?"

Holy cow, was that a door opening in the wall of her defenses? "Lady, you're the one who wouldn't return my calls after we got naked in my bass boat."

"And you weren't itching to run?"

Well, she had him there. He cupped her face. "I think we were both rocked by more than the trailer's suspension."

"You have the most wonderful way of making me smile when I need it."

He thumbed her cheekbone and thought of how easy it would be to seduce her into the bed behind her, but the request had to come from her. He let his hands drop to his sides. "Where's your toolbox?"

She stepped back. "I have one up here in the hall closet from the last time I removed the sink drain."

"You removed the drain?" Was there anything this woman couldn't handle on her own? Other than an air conditioner.

"The pipes are small. It had a bad clog."

"Of course."

Claire handled life. He admired that about her, even if that confidence came with a prickly pride. Smoothing that pride came with its benefits.

She came back into the room just as he stripped his T-shirt over his head.

Her eyes went wide, then scorched over him in a thorough glide that hitched on his bared chest, lower to his running shorts, which weren't going to provide much camo for his arousal if he didn't turn around ASAP.

Whoa, baby, Claire's starved hormones gasped as she stared at bare-chested Vic, then the broad expanse of his back as he turned away to work on her AC.

Maybe she would have been better off letting him hire a repairman after all, because keeping her hands to herself would be tougher than resurrecting her decrepit air conditioner. It had been a long week being near him, hearing his footsteps in her house and life, but not touching him. So many times she'd stood on the edge of asking him back into her room, but things had been going so well she was afraid of losing that growing bond.

Or so she'd told herself over and over again. Yet standing alone in a room with him, a bed and minimal clothes, she weakened. Caution slipped away. Would it always be like this for them?

Right now she couldn't think of a single reason they shouldn't be together. She wanted to roll with him in her sheets while wind blew through the window and the ceiling fan clicked overhead. Just as they'd done nearly four months ago, out of control. Only with Vic did she loosen the rigid restraints of her daily regimen.

Then she couldn't think at all, because somehow they were kissing. She didn't know who'd moved first, couldn't even recall either of them walking, just the meeting and mating of mouths. The smell of sweat on his slick skin, the salty taste of him as she sketched her lips along the bold line of his collarbone. Her T-shirt went up and over her head, whipping a gust of air over her bared flesh as it sailed to rest on her chaise.

Vic growled his appreciation. "No underwear."

"Let's see about you." She hitched her fingers in his running shorts and swept them down over the taut curve of his butt. He kicked the clothes free and clasped her to him, the rigid length of him a steely pressure against her stomach. The ceiling fan swished lazy whispers over her passion-fired skin.

Nipping down her neck, he sauntered around her side to her back, looping his arm around front. "Are you ready for another position?"

"Where should we—"

"Right here." He clasped her wrists and placed her hands against the towering bedpost. "Hold on."

She gripped the smooth expanse of polished wood, sturdy, steady, like the towering man behind her, stepping closer, covering her. The heat of him melded to her back as she nestled her bottom more firmly against his stomach.

His arm linked around her, he dipped his fingers between her legs, spreading her wider, readying her with coaxing circles. Her nerves already taut, tingled hotter with each slick stroke of his fingers.

"Enough," she gasped, wondering if there would ever be enough of this with him.

He shifted against her, positioning, the thick length of him prodding, then filling her. She stretched her arms higher in synch with her moan, her fingers digging into the carved pattern of the post.

"Okay?"

"Better than okay. Don't stop."

"As long as you can hold on." His hands moved up to cradle her breasts, tugging, rolling her nipples as he moved inside her with sure but shallow thrusts, ever careful of her condition, teasing and pleasing all at once.

Claire ground back against him, seeking… more, an end to the torment clenching inside her, a hunger she wasn't sure would ever go away completely, which scared her. Because then she needed him. Just him. Wanting was one thing. Need was something else altogether.

But oh, how she needed release, couldn't remember a time she'd been this desperate to…

She bit back a scream, pressed her forehead to the post, her mouth against her wrist muffling the echoes of her satisfaction she couldn't restrain.

His muscled arms banded around her, catching her against him as she shivered. A thrust later, he shuddered, his hoarse groan vibrating against her ear. Thank goodness his legs seemed to have a bit more substance than hers at the moment or they would both be on the floor.

Again he lifted her, effortlessly, and placed her in the middle of the giving softness of her comforter and stretched alongside her. A rumbling sounded from her window a second before the air conditioner resurrected, chugging sub-arctic blasts over her sweat-slicked body. Superstitious Starr would have called the surprise repair a sign to trust in miracles and Vic.

And at the moment, with his baby just beginning to flutter inside her, Claire wanted more than ever to be a little like her sister and believe in miracles.

Finally, he was in Claire's lilac-scented bedroom again—a flipping miracle, one he didn't want to screw up.

Stretched on her frou-frou chaise, Claire between his legs and leaning back against his chest, he toyed with a lock of her hair, spent. He didn't have much time to cement the moment. If only tomorrow were a Monday, her day off as well as his, and they could laze in the tangled sheets all day, make love a couple more times. He was running out of vacation days. In fact, had to be on call now to make up for all the days off to romance Claire. Apparently the time had been well spent even if he'd felt like they were treading water all week.

Vic checked his cellphone on the end table and willed it to stay silent, most definitely no calls from Mrs. Bethea about Trooper now.

Seesawing the strand of Claire's hair between his fingers, he studied all the colors twining through, as complex as the woman herself. "What's with the rocks?"

He nodded to the rows of mason jars packed with colorful stones he'd been too enamored with her body to ask about the other times he'd been in her room. Now, he needed the distraction of conversation to drag his attention off that bed.

"What do you mean?"

"You have jars of them all over the house."

"I'm a cheapskate decorator, and I'm broke to boot."

"And you're also a prideful woman feeding me a line. Are the rocks some secret?"

She tipped her head against his shoulder to smile up at him. "It's a piece of me, I guess, and we both know I can be a little stingy with sharing those." She looked down and away. "When I was a kid I collected unique or pretty rocks that caught my eye. Every time we left a place, I took my favorite from that home with me, something familiar so I wouldn't feel so lost in the new place."

No wonder this house was important to her. He'd been attached to the house he grew up in but selling the place had been a relief. He'd put a few pieces of furniture in storage. The rest had gone to his sister or been donated to the church.

Claire had been given so little she collected rocks.

He wanted to haul her up and take her on a

shopping spree to fill her house with all the things no one had given her. And what about the things she needed beyond her house, in her life? The woman fought him tooth and nail over fixing an air conditioner.

Because you couldn't lose what you didn't have.

He of all people should have realized that facet to her pride. "So you lugged all these rocks with you when you moved in?"

Her laugh vibrated her back against his chest. "I didn't have so many then, just a sack full. When I looked at those rocks, I remembered Tina—my mother—and the things we'd done together. Before I knew it, I was picking up rocks anytime Aunt Libby and I did something special so I would have a way to remember her when I left."

"But you didn't leave here."

"No, I didn't."

Claire hadn't gone home to her mother or

been adopted. What a limbo life for a kid. Just thinking of Emma having existed that way—he couldn't picture it. But somehow Claire had, still turning into the strong, successful woman he held at the moment.

She scratched her fingers lightly along his chest, back and forth. "Don't you want to know if one of those rocks has your name on it?"

He hadn't even considered the possibility. "I would like that very much."

"The day I met you. Do you remember?"

A test? Easy enough because he remembered it well. "You were painting your porch."

"I looked like hell."

"You looked natural and cute with a paint speckle on your nose."

"Starr and I were stenciling shells along the inside of the railing." The curtains fluffed out around them with puffs from her air conditioner. "People always notice Starr first. Even if they disapprove, they see her, then they notice me, usually when they get hungry. And I'm totally okay with that. I don't particularly like being the center of attention as long as I'm in charge."

If she truly thought she faded into the background around Starr, Claire was big-time mistaken.

He tweaked a strand of her hair. "Really? You like being in charge? I never would have guessed." His hands trekked to palm her breasts. "I definitely noticed you."

She chuckled, sending an elbow lightly back into his gut. "You gave Starr a polite hello over your shoulder, but your attention stayed on me and wow, was my attention ever on you."

Yeah, he remembered it pretty much the same way. He also remembered how shaken to his boots he was by a sucker punch he couldn't remember ever having experienced in his life. Certain then he would never marry again, he'd told himself this was definitely a woman he needed to keep firmly on the friendship side. Stepping over that line would be dangerous.

He'd been completely right.

Claire scooched from between his legs to the end of the chaise, standing, gloriously naked, any self-consciousness over her pregnant body rightfully gone. She crossed to her bedside table, with a clock, a lamp filled with shells, and bowl full of stones. She clinked through, plucking out a paint-speckled rock.

She displayed it in the palm of her hand. "Silly, huh?"

He swung his feet over the edge, sitting to face her, drawing her between his knees. He cupped her hand in his, folding their fingers together over the stone. "Not silly at all. Our kid will like that story someday."

"That's a really sweet thought." She rested her other hand on top of his. "What story did Emma like best?"

He pulled up the memory, surprised it didn't

burn as much as he would have expected. In fact it even made him smile. "A book called *The Paper Bag Princess,* about a tough little girl who doesn't need a prince to save her."

She cradled his face in her hands. "I'm glad you're the father of my baby."

A wall full of diplomas didn't mean as much to him as that one compliment. "We're going to make this work, Claire."

He skimmed a knuckle over her lips conveniently at eye level, and hey, what do ya know, mouth level, too. He angled toward her—

His cellphone rang from beside the bed.

Groaning, he rested his forehead in the crook of her neck for two ragged breaths before he shoved to his feet. She snatched the phone up, passing it to him. The office. Hell.

Three minutes later, he thumbed the off button while Claire finished pulling his shirt over her head.

He stifled a curse over the abrupt end to their

evening just when it seemed he was making progress with her. "I have to head out. A mare in labor and she's had a difficult time in the past. They want a vet on hand. I'll try my best to be back in time for your big event tonight, then I hope we can pick up where we left off."

"Me, too." She shot him a slow, sexy smile.

He hated to wipe that look off her face, but it couldn't be avoided. "Swear you'll call Starr's guy friend to keep an eye on things."

Her smile downgraded to half-power, but at least stayed partially in place. "He's not nearly as much fun as having you around."

"I should hope not." He dropped a quick kiss on her lips, all he could allow himself and still manage to get out of her house before sunrise. "I really do need to shower off fast and go."

In her bathroom, he cranked on the shower, stepping under the spray before it warmed. A wise idea if he planned to face the world anytime soon. He yanked the curtain that encircled the old-fashioned tub, and reached to her high window ledge to snag her shampoo and a bar of soap.

The small rectangular window glowed with the moon illuminating more of those rocks in clear apothecary jars and even tiny dishes. She could really use a stone fountain outside to collect some of these into one place. Maybe he could scout out a rock from somewhere they'd been together. Women went gaga over sentimentality, right?

Through the rush of water and his plans, he heard a ringing in his ears. A phone. His cellphone again. Not another one. "Could you get that for me and take a message?"

"Sure."

"Thanks." Shoving his head back under the warming spray, he swept his hands over his face and hair, sluicing away the shampoo and soap.

The bathroom door opened the rest of the way, Claire filling the portal. His eyes caught on the lush beauty of her in his T-shirt, elegant even in worn cotton. Cotton he intended to peel up and off so she could join him in the shower. He searched his mind for a fresh position to try out with her. God, he enjoyed her adventurous spirit when it came to sex. Perhaps they could just spend their life together working their way through the Kama sutra.

Starting with plastering her back to the shower wall while he hitched her leg over his arm.

"Claire." Just *Claire*. He let how much he wanted her come through in that one hoarsely spoken syllable.

When she didn't move toward him or speak, alarms sounded in his head and he looked up to her face. Her expressionless face.

Mental alarms cranked to full volume. Something had gone way wrong in the past fifteen seconds.

She extended her arm, his cellphone in hand. "It's your ex-wife."

Ten

Vic's wife.

Ex. Ex. *Ex*-wife, Claire reminded herself.

She gripped the banister on her way down the stretch of stairs overlooking the hallway hostess station and gift shop. The green-eyed monster might be nipping her heels, but she refused to let the little devil take her down.

All the same, Sonya's call made for a serious mood buster. Claire had showered off in the spare bathroom rather than sit around waiting while Vic's voice rumbled through his conversation with a woman he'd once loved. The door ajar had given too tempting a peek at his reflection in the mirror, towel around his slim waist, moisture clinging to his body begging to be licked off.

Except he'd been talking to his ex-wife on his cellphone.

Darn it. No denying, she *was* jealous, even though she knew, knew, totally knew he didn't love the woman anymore.

So she'd hidden under the shower spray rather than do something as juvenile as eavesdrop. As he was leaving, he'd called out to her while she was dressing. She'd pretended nothing was wrong—no surrendering to the green monster—and she'd hollered a farewell.

She didn't like all these disorderly emotions.

Claire stepped onto the first floor, sweeping aside curtains and cranking open windows to reveal the rest of the world rousing at the crack of dawn. Through the windows, she saw David Reis with his mother on their terrace, Starr watching from her porch with a mug of something steaming. Ronnie Calhoun gutting a grouper fish on the long wooden table with a sink and hose outside his seafood shop at the marina.

Vic's truck pulling out onto the main road.

Even from a distance she could see his broad shoulders through the rear window sporting his Cornell alumni sticker. Such a complex man, successful and in charge with a quiet confidence. It wasn't just about sex and the moment. It couldn't be.

And she so didn't have the time to sort through this, even with her self-imposed deadline looming. She needed to get to work preparing the lunch menu before the doors opened at eleven. If she and her sisters could afford to hire more help, they could add breakfast hours as well. The rehearsal party tonight would go a long way toward taking them out of the red, and more importantly, spreading the word about their cuisine.

This particular bridal party consisted of no less than a dozen bridesmaids, representing twelve of Charleston's wealthiest families. The groom's family had paid for all the extras in an attempt to impress the bride's influential relatives.

The doorbell droned through the house—the low, long buzzer of the backdoor, not the chimes of the front. She startled, hating that she had to be so on edge from the prowler incident. This early, that bell meant fresh catch arriving. Nothing to worry about.

She had plenty to keep her occupied. She liked staying busy, less time to think.

Her steps slowed.

Less time to think? Where had that come from? She prided herself on her logic and organization, so why was she running so hard from reason now when it mattered most?

The truth whispered through her like the

magnolia-and-ocean-scented breeze billowing her curtains. Because her brain echoed her heart and her heart spoke clearly, now that she was standing still long enough to listen.

She loved Vic Jansen. And tonight after she clicked off the last light from the party, she would have to figure out what to do with all these feelings that screamed at her to pitch reason and caution into the harbor.

Moonlight streaking through the oak and palm trees, Vic sprinted down the street lined with parked cars leading to Beachcombers. He couldn't even get to his flipping garage with all the traffic tonight—a combination of regular restaurant clientele and the big rehearsal dinner.

If these cars were anything to judge by, the gas leak hadn't slowed business a bit. Claire and her sisters could celebrate their unqualified success.

He wished he could have finished earlier to

help, but he'd had an essential errand to run. A surprise for her. And he also knew Claire could manage on her own. She would make a helluva partner in business.

And in a marriage. Yeah, the *M* word still spooked him, but the call from hyper-needy Sonya made him realize more than ever how lucky he was to have this second chance with Claire. Now he had to convince her the call from his ex had meant nothing, because only an idiot would think it wouldn't bother her, especially this early in their relationship.

He would take Claire on a starlit walk alongside the ocean and propose again—the right way this time. With a diamond engagement ring he'd bought this afternoon.

Vic patted the pocket of his jeans on his way up the dock to clean up. A guy shouldn't propose smelling like a horse.

A quick trip to his boat later, he'd showered off and changed into khakis and a polo shirt. He vaulted up on deck only to stop short at the shadowy figure lounging in the captain's chair.

His muscles bunched a second before his eyes adjusted to the dim dock lights enough to make out his brother-in-law's features. "Hey, Bo, what are you doing here?"

"Kirstie's at a sleepover." His brother-in-law leaned back. "Since Paige doesn't get home from her nursing school conference until tomorrow, I decided to snag a bite here and check out what's going on with my buddy Joker's rehearsal dinner. I saw you jog by— parking sucks, doesn't it?—and thought we could catch up."

The ring burned a hole in his pocket. Nearly forty years old, he shouldn't be this edgy about proposing. He knew what he was doing was right, and still something felt…off? "How is everything going with the party?"

"Seems great. Folks are raving about the food, and of course, the service rocks."

Just as he would expect from Claire. God, he was proud of her and happy for her.

His brother-in-law studied him with a too-probing stare. "Do you want to talk about what's been bothering you this week?"

The ring grew heavy in his pocket. "I think maybe I do."

Bo's eyebrows soared toward his hairline. "Really?"

"What?" Vic dropped into the seat across from his brother-in-law, the gentle slap of waves against the dock providing none of its usual calming effect. "I talk."

"Sure, you talk, and you listen especially well." He lounged back on his elbows. "You offer up great advice that I have appreciated on more than one occasion when it comes to figuring out your sister, but I can't think of a time you've asked for anyone else's."

That couldn't be right. Vic thumbed salt spray

off gauges. And if it was, he didn't like what it said about him.

"No insult meant, dude," Bo assured. "It's just that you're very much the typical oldest, take charge, fix problems. Of course that comes with the baggage of feeling responsible for the world."

Vic couldn't stop himself from checking Beachcombers, searching. For problems?

Or Claire.

Then there she was, at the door passing out something from a large basket hooked over her arm. Party favors, maybe? Some kind of wedding commemoration for the happy couple.

Damn, she was amazing, so smooth and beautiful in her poise. Her strength. He couldn't let her get away.

He turned back to Bo. "You're not helping me here."

His brother-in-law grinned. "You haven't actually asked for any specific advice."

The guy had a point that sounded a lot like

something Claire had said to him about him always telling rather than asking. "Claire's pregnant."

"Well, uh—" Bo's jaw worked up and down a few times, before he just grinned and extended his hand. "Congratulations, dude."

"Thanks." Vic grimaced. "Although you may want to hold off on that. I haven't been able to convince her to marry me yet, and I could use some advice on tipping the odds in my favor."

"How hard have you tried?"

That was a little insulting. "I've been trying all week long."

And why not the past few months? No wonder she doubted him.

"Just commenting on your usually top-notch focus. A cross-country move?" Bo snapped his fingers. "No problem. You even snag a coveted partnership in a practice that other area vets have been jockeying to nab for years. Whatever you want, you make it happen."

"I couldn't keep my daughter alive." Where had that come from? Still, the reality stabbed at him, the guilt.

The pain.

Hearing from Sonya this morning must have messed with his head more than he'd thought.

His eyes gravitated back to Claire finishing with the last of the party guests. Claire, carrying his kid. Everything he wanted right there.

"Dude." Bo leaned forward, knees on elbows, easygoing smile long gone. "You've got to stop blaming yourself. You have a real chance here to be happy, build a life, and you're gonna screw it up. Women have this freaky weird way of sensing when a guy's only half with them. You need to haul your butt a hundred percent into this second chance you've been given or she's always gonna wonder if you're marrying her for the baby."

No freaking kidding.

But something else Bo said niggled at his head.

Only half here. Hadn't he wondered the same thing about himself more than once over the past few years? He just hadn't thought the rest of the world noticed that he'd only been going through the motions since Emma died, adrift, rudderless, because the thought of losing everything again... Damn. "Why didn't you mention this before?"

"Nothing worse—or less effective—than unsolicited advice."

"Valid point." Vic clapped his brother-in-law on the shoulder. "Thanks for the help."

Bo thumped him back. "And thank *you* for not beating the crap out of me because I sleep with your sister."

Vic scowled—sorta. "Don't push your luck."

Luck.

Yeah, some of life boiled down to luck, but a man increased his odds with sweat equity. And heaven knew when he hauled his butt—and his heart—one hundred percent into this relationship, he would be sweating the outcome big time.

* * *

Claire swiped her wrist over her sweaty forehead, morning sickness back with a vengeance long after dark on one of the most important days of her life. At least she'd held off until the last rehearsal party guest drove away. She only needed to store the leftovers and clean up.

Her sister had the bar crowd well in hand, kitchen closed for the night. Even if it was a mess. Claire plucked another peppermint from her apron pocket and popped it in her mouth to settle her stomach.

She sagged to sit at the table, old beach music tunes thrumming from the bar's sound system through the wall. Romantic, sappy songs about dancing barefoot in the sand with the one you love. She would just rest her head for a few minutes until the candy dissolved. Her eyes drifted closed and lethargy basted over her, music lulling her, conjuring dream images…

A door swished a second before a light

streaked across the kitchen from the other room, but she was too tired to look up. "Starr, I added Southwest spices to the party mix and it's in the pantry, second shelf from the bottom, container's marked. I added extra peanuts like you asked, and I'm sorry for not bringing it out like I promised."

A chair scraped back beside her, followed by the creak of someone sitting. "It's me."

Vic. She wished she had the energy to look up at him, but it was all she could do to keep her food in her stomach. The aftertaste of grilled shrimp curdled in her mouth, even past the peppermint. If she could conquer the nausea enough to sleep, then everything would be fine in the morning. She wanted to snuggle up beside him and drift off, but they'd left things so unsettled earlier.

Or rather, she had by hiding in the shower because she was too scared to admit she totally loved this man. She should tell him. This was their deadline night, after all. But *sheesh,* would he even believe her given her limp-rag enthusiasm?

She raised her leaden head and some of her exhaustion eased. Oh, he looked good, his blond hair damp and darker from a shower. The sky-blue polo shirt echoed the color of his eyes and as tired as she was, she wanted to just enjoy the view, while his baby fluttered inside her.

Popping another peppermint in her mouth, she clicked it to the side against her teeth. "Did everything go all right with the emergencies?"

"Don't you want to know why Sonya phoned?"

No beating around the bush.

Yes, she wanted to know. And no, maybe not. "You were married to her. You have a connection through your past. As you said yourself, that's not a bond you would take lightly."

"There is no bond anymore." He leaned forward, his forearms on the table, muscles flexing and filling short sleeves. "The problems that broke us up would have surfaced eventually. Losing Emma only brought everything to the front faster."

"Problems?" She ached to know, ached too much. She held up her hands and tried to ignore the tempting press of his knee against hers. "Never mind. Forget I asked. I sound like some jealous woman."

"You have a right to be."

"I have reason to be jealous?" The ache doubled.

"No." He leaned closer, the scent of soap and his shower heavy in the air. "I said you have a right, but no reason."

She couldn't miss his intensity, the honesty. Excitement and yes, anxiety, fizzed, bubbles expanding inside her from the pressure of her emotions.

"Sonya called because our old church has collected money for a memorial for Emma, and Sonya wanted to know what to do with the fund."

The fizz went flat with guilt. What an emotional phone conversation that must have been and she'd been hiding out in her shower. Vic deserved so much better than that from her. She couldn't change this morning, but she would offer better now.

Claire reached across to clasp his hand, squeezing hard and wondering how to squeeze hard enough against a pain that intense. Thinking about anything happening to her baby sent her stomach churning faster. "What did you say to Sonya?"

He shrugged his broad shoulders that carried the load for everyone. "I told her to buy some new playground equipment for the church." His throat moved with a long swallow. "Emma would have enjoyed that."

Her own throat closed with more of those messy emotions, because darn it all, life was messy sometimes. She had to hold him. What she should have done this morning, except she'd been too busy battling her pride.

"I'm so sorry for not being there after you hung up the phone." She started to stand, but her stomach rebelled at the quick movement. She grabbed the table for support.

"Claire?" He kicked back his chair.

Words of reassurance snagged in her throat. She tried to straighten, but…omigod. Her stomach cramped. Unrelenting.

Her baby.

Fiery pain lanced through her belly, fear stabbing her heart as well. She doubled over, her vision pulling into a tight pinpoint. Her knees turned noodle-weak and she sagged toward the floor, Vic's hoarse shout of denial fading with consciousness.

Eleven

Pacing outside the E.R. exam room, Vic stomped down the denial still roaring through him. He couldn't be about to lose Claire and the baby. The horror of watching her keel over crashed through him again. He'd caught her, telling himself this was nothing more than exhaustion, like a week ago.

Except when she'd woken, rather than being woozy, she'd cried out, clutching her stomach.

He hadn't been willing to wait around for an

ambulance. Instead, he'd carried her to his truck and raced to the nearest hospital, all the while refusing to believe the past could repeat itself.

Trying to save someone he loved.

Failing.

What a helluva time to realize he loved Claire. Really loved her.

Bo had been right about getting his butt one hundred percent into this relationship. He'd been so intent on winning her over through determination, then calculated romance, he'd lost sight of the emotions, the most important part.

Yes, he loved her and he would never forgive himself if he'd missed out on the chance to tell her. That it had taken him this long to figure it out made him realize she'd been right to refuse his proposal before. Pretending the past week had been about duty and friendship hadn't kept his heart one bit safer.

The antiseptic air stung his nose as he paced around stark institutional furniture. He hated hospitals after those awful hours when they'd hoped maybe Emma would make it…. He thought about calling Bo to come hang out with him. He could also get Starr and Reis back up from the coffee shop easily enough. Except all he wanted waited on the other side of that exam room door.

Staring at that double panel, he willed himself to stay steady for Claire in case she needed him. His heart jackhammered against his ribs. He jammed his fist into his pocket, bumping up against the velvet ring box.

The doors swished open, the resident on call striding through scribbling on a chart. The room went quiet or maybe it was just because he was so intent on—

"Dr. Jansen?"

"Yes?" Vic steeled himself. "How's Claire? How's the baby?"

"I can't give you details since you're not the next of kin, but suffice it to say they're both going to be fine."

Relief turned his vision hazy. And damn it, he would do everything in his power to change his status as next of kin as soon as he took Claire home.

The young doc flipped the pages back in order on the chart board. "Ms. McDermott is asking for you and can fill you in on the specifics."

The last of the doctor's speech barely registered since at the words "asking for you," Vic sprinted toward the swishing doors.

Claire smiled weakly from the gurney, an IV attached to her arm. She certainly didn't look okay to him in her hospital gown, blanket draped over her legs. In fact, she looked like hell. Pale, drawn, bathed in stark halogen lights.

"Food poisoning," she whispered.

Food poisoning? At Claire's restaurant. Holy crap. No wonder she looked ill through and through. If this spread to other patrons…

Her smile faded altogether. "I could be out

of business for good. The bad luck just continues, huh?"

He linked hands with her. "The way I see it, your luck's holding just fine. You're okay and the baby's okay. Let's worry about the rest later. Right now, you two are the most important thing."

"Of course. I want to go home, but the doctor said I need to stay overnight on the IV to make sure I don't dehydrate."

Overnight? He might hate hospitals, but nothing could pry him from the property.

Starr burst through the door in a whirlwind of wild curls and concern. "Thank goodness you're awake and well. And the bambino, too. I swear you are not going to snow me anymore about how you're doing fine. I'm going to nail horseshoes for luck all around your room and you're not getting out of bed until I say…"

Her voice droned on with sisterly concern as he slumped back against a supply cabinet to drag in air for his galloping pulse. The ruckus in his ears intensified until he could have sworn there was a riot outside.

He swept open the door to locate a nurse to control the noise so Claire could rest peacefully—and found a mob crowding the waiting area. A mob full of familiar faces, people he'd passed while jogging by all those parked cars at Claire's.

The huge wedding party from the rehearsal dinner milled around, groaning. All pale. The groom—Bo's buddy—raced for the bathroom behind the nurse's station.

Something had definitely gone wrong with the food at Beachcombers. Vic released the door, muffling the commotion.

"Vic?" Claire asked.

He had to be honest. She would find out anyhow soon enough and would need the time to troubleshoot. "Most of the wedding party is out there signing in."

Puking their guts up. But she didn't need that much detail.

She covered her mouth with a trembling hand. "Our food?"

"But Starr's not sick." He turned to Claire's sister. "Are you?"

Starr shook her head, curls bouncing. "Not a bit."

Claire elbowed up with a wince and crinkle of liner paper. "I was having one of those finicky craving moments and filled up on shrimp, so I had Starr taste everything else."

"Shrimp." Starr chewed her lip gloss off. "It's the only thing I didn't eat. But it could have simply been left out too long by accident."

"Accident, my ass," Vic bit out. "Not a chance would methodical Claire have left anything out for too long."

Claire slumped back on the pillow, her eyes going pensive with that lining-up-facts look of hers he recognized well. "Ronnie Calhoun sold us that shrimp. A mistake like that could put him out of business."

He picked up her logic thread. "Or maybe he was trying to close down yours, and has been working at it for weeks now." The answer felt…right. And if the guess was right, that bastard Calhoun was going down. "There were saw cuts under your porch and now we know where to look for a matching blade, which, if we're lucky will still have sawdust residue from your deck. Maybe we'll luck into a footprint match from that lurking incident."

Claire grabbed his wrist. "Where are you going?"

Vic held up his cellphone. "Outside to call the cops about paying a visit to Ronnie Calhoun."

Endlessly practical Claire had never needed his help—heaven knows, she would never ask for it—but he could do this for her and the business that meant so much to her. Damn straight, his whole world was in that tiny exam room and he wasn't letting anyone threaten his second chance.

Outside her house the next morning, Claire clasped the armrest in Vic's truck after an all clear from her doctor. She hadn't even considered riding home with her sister. That spoke volumes about her where her heart and loyalty lay these days, but she knew now it was time to step forward into her future.

She and Vic were a couple. She hoped his feelings ran as deeply as hers, but regardless, she wanted to build something with him. Risky? Most certainly, especially for someone who'd never stepped out on a ledge before. But she'd learned a lot about bravery from watching how he rebuilt his life.

Relaxing back in the seat, she tried not to worry about the lunch crowd—or if they would even have one. Starr and Ashley had everything in hand. They might not serve everything the way she would, but she was learning to take life as it came, another gift from Vic.

She thought about the evening before and winged a grateful prayer for her baby's health. A whispery kick reassured her. "I feel so badly for messing up that poor couple's rehearsal dinner. Were they too ill to get married today?"

"The groom's still hooked up to a hydrating IV, and the bride hit the road."

"She walked out on him? You're serious?" Apparently relationships were tough all the way around these days.

"According to the gossip, the bride got cold feet. She called his hospital room to let him know she was safe, but not planning to come back since his military life was too stressful for her. Of course, life doesn't come with guarantees no matter what job you're in."

And wasn't that the truth. She was counting her blessings today. Vic stopped short of the marina parking lot.

A cop car waited outside her home—again. But they were here for Ronnie Calhoun this time, thank goodness. And double thanks that they were investigating so quickly. David Reis had already placed a call to a connection of his at the police station to make sure the facts of this case were leaked to the press. The press would be far more likely to print the whole deal if they felt they'd gotten a scoop from the cops. That should clear Beachcombers from negative fallout.

Vic's jaw flexed so hard she feared he would crack a crown. Rather than pull all the way into the marina parking lot, he stopped outside her place and made it around to her side of the truck before she could so much as set one foot out the door.

Ronnie Calhoun glared at them from a hundred yards away. She could see the guilt stamped all over him from across the patchy beach lawn. Relief surged through her to think that the cops would soon have evidence to pin him.

She rested her hand on Vic's arm. "Let's just go inside."

As she turned, a flash snagged her attention. Ronnie's silly old captain's hat sailing off his head. Because he was running.

Charging in her direction with fury on his face. "You uppity bitch!"

The startled cop reached to grab the out-of-control man by the shoulder.

Ronnie wrenched free with frenetic strength. Hurtling over a gardenia bush, the wiry sailor launched himself toward her with his fist raised. Her arms closed protectively around her stomach, her child, Vic's child.

She stumbled backward. Swept by the power of strong hands. Vic stepped in front of her, blocking the madman from her path and giving the cops enough time to subdue him again. As much as she prided herself on her independence, she had to admit it felt good to have someone to lean on right now, someone to stand with her in protecting their child.

Ronnie Calhoun was no competition for the man who handled nine-hundred-pound horses.

The crazed marina owner jerked in the police officers' grasps. "Why couldn't you have just taken the money and moved?" he garbled, spittle bubbling along with his venom. "I wouldn't have plowed the house. I would have run a classy operation, a bigger one, with more prestige."

His fanatical anger slowly shifted to outright panic, his movements now as twitchy as the hummingbird zipping around her azalea bushes. He looked around as if only just realizing there were other people around besides her.

Ronnie Calhoun had made a serious mistake.

He cranked his head to look back at the cops. "I want a deal. I'll tell you anything. I want a deal so I can come home."

Through it all, Vic stayed in front of her,

wordlessly, but the tendons bulging in his neck spoke volumes.

Ronnie's neurotic ramblings faded as the cops loaded him into their cruiser.

Tension seeped from Vic's shoulders. Turning, he locked his arms around her as she shivered over how close she'd lived to a maniac all this time. She relaxed against him, confident she could lean against him.

A rock.

How many times had she thought that about him without making the connection to her collection?

Vic was as immovable as a boulder, sure, but always right beside her. A man she could lean on and count on, and he always had been. She'd just been too caught up in the past to see the oh-so-logical truth in front of her. She didn't need to collect cold chips of earth to hold her memories anymore.

She had a hot-blooded, breathing man to

stand by her side and make living memories with. Better yet, make plans for the future. Their future.

Together.

Once the cop cruiser with Calhoun inside disappeared around the corner, Vic stepped back from Claire and held out his hand. His purpose was set now, thanks to a good swift kick in the pants from life—and the helpful prod of his brother-in-law's advice.

Thanks to this amazing woman in front of him, he'd also learned that asking sometimes worked better than ordering. "Do you need help with the stairs?"

Vic nodded toward the walkway lined with flowering azaleas to her house. Hopefully his home soon, too. He wanted to talk to her, but had to wait for the right time. She was a woman well worth waiting for.

She placed her hand in his, the hanging

baskets of ferns swaying and creaking with the breeze rolling in off the ocean. "I'm feeling pretty good, actually. I would like to sit out on the dock, if you don't mind, before it gets too hot."

Neutral ground, not her house, not his boat. Just the two of them out in the open. Maybe the time had come to talk after all.

"If you're sure. But I swear if you so much as stumble, I'm carrying you back up to the house."

A serene—and sexy as hell—smile dimpled her cheeks. "Like that's a threat?"

His arm slid around her waist as they strolled past the meticulously lined-up shells along the edges of the dock. He enjoyed nudging her world off-kilter every now and again, just as he appreciated the order she brought to his world.

Her back went stiff against his arm. Unease itched at the thought of being given the boot after all now that her deadline had arrived.

She wrapped her arms around her stomach,

keeping stride slowly, her face studiedly forward. "I had a lot of time to mull things over, lying in that hospital bed, and I was thinking we could string a hammock from a couple of the trees in the section of yard between Beach-combers and the carriage house."

Exhaling his relief, he hugged her closer, soft curves fitting perfectly. "Those live oaks look sturdy enough. You'll enjoy that."

"No. I meant for you." She tipped her face to look up at him, her eyes as open and vulnerable as he'd ever seen them, prideful, prickly Claire apparently nervous and wanting this as much as he did. "Maybe you could even catch naps there with the baby sometimes in our yard."

Our yard. Still, he wanted to make sure they went into this on even footing. He needed an equal partnership from the get-go. "I meant what I said about not being a kept man."

"I could see my way clear to relenting on some of the financial issues. I mean, after all, the neighborhood will be saying you married me for my hot body, right?"

Married.

He stilled, staring deep into her chocolate-brown eyes, rich with emotion. Well, hell. She'd beaten him to the punch on proposing and knocked him right off his moorings with her unexpected suggestion. Not to mention her acceptance of his need to contribute.

Her shaky smile strengthened. "I assume your offer is still open to spend our lives together, beachcombing for shells and memories together with our child."

"And sometimes just the two of us."

"I would like that."

At the end of the pier, he sat with her on the hardwood bench. He searched for the words to get this right, to convince her that he would have come to this point in their relationship even if there had been no baby.

He thought of how she'd been such a quiet,

steady support when he'd told her about the memorial for Emma. "I lost people I loved, and because of that I let myself stop needing anyone. At the time it seemed easier. Safer." He shook his head. "Somehow it didn't work out the way I planned, thanks to you. It's one thing to lose because of fickle fate. But if I lose you because of my own pigheaded stupidity… I don't think I can get over that."

She bracketed his face in her hands. "You're not going to lose me. You should know by now what a stubborn woman I am. It may take me a while to reason everything out, but once I make up my mind, I'm there."

He cupped the back of her neck. "You jumped ahead of me with the hammock, but I've been giving a lot of thought to your rocks and how each one commemorates a special moment in your life."

"How romantic. Yes, we need to head back to the yard to find a rock." Grinning, she started to stand. "Or maybe a special shell will do, totally different and distinguishable."

"Hold on." He tapped her shoulder and eased her back to the bench. "Actually, the rock I have in mind is already here."

He shifted from the bench to kneel in front of her on the hard-planked pier, the perfect place to propose with the morning sun streaming over her.

He held out his hand, ring box between two fingers. "I love you, Claire, and if you'll let me, I would like to be your rock for the rest of our lives. Just as I know I can depend on you to be mine."

Tears glinted in her eyes. "Yes. I will marry you. And yes, I love you, too, so very much, and would be honored to stand by your side, have your children, share your bed and life."

He urged her forward as he leaned to meet her. Yeah, he could picture forever spent kissing this lady, mussing up her hair in her big bed or one of his boats.

As his wife.

She extended her hand, her left, in an unmistakable invitation. He'd never thought he could do this again, but then he never could have imagined a woman as perfect for him as Claire.

He plucked the engagement ring from the box and guided it into place on Claire's finger.

She lifted her hand, the morning sun catching the stone and casting sparks onto the dark, shadowy water lapping at the dock. "Wow, that's quite a rock."

"You're quite a lady."

She stared back at him, her eyes glistening with more of those tears as bright as the sparks off her ring. "You really do love me."

Yeah, he did. And he looked forward to reminding her for the rest of their lives. "Baby, I've been yours since the first time I saw you with paint on your perfect nose."

* * * * *